The Great Prince Shan

The Great Prince Shan

E. Phillips Oppenheim

MINT EDITIONS

The Great Prince Shan was first published in 1922.

This edition published by Mint Editions 2021.

ISBN 9781513281223 | E-ISBN 9781513286242

Published by Mint Editions®

 MINT
EDITIONS

minteditionbooks.com

Publishing Director: Jennifer Newens
Design & Production: Rachel Lopez Metzger
Project Manager: Micaela Clark
Typesetting: Westchester Publishing Services

Contents

I

A club for diplomats and gentlemen," Prince Karschoff remarked, looking lazily through a little cloud of tobacco smoke around the spacious but almost deserted card room. "The classification seems comprehensive enough, yet it seems impossible to get even a decent rubber of bridge."

Sir Daniel Harker, a many years retired plenipotentiary to one of the smaller Powers, shrugged his shoulders.

"Personally, I have come to the conclusion," he declared, "that the *raison d'être* for the club seems to be passing. There is no diplomacy, nowadays, and every man who pays his taxes is a gentleman. Kingley, you are the youngest. Ransack the club and find a fourth."

The Honourable Nigel Kingley smiled lazily from the depths of his easy-chair. He was a young Englishman of normal type, long-limbed, clean-shaven, with good features, a humorous mouth and keen grey eyes.

"In actual years," he admitted, "I may have the advantage of you two, but so far as regards the qualities of youth, Karschoff is the youngest man here. Besides, no one could refuse him anything."

"It is a subterfuge," the Prince objected, "but if I must go, I will go presently. We will wait five minutes, in case Providence should be kind to us."

The three men relapsed into silence. They were seated in a comfortable recess of the card room of the St. Philip's Club. The atmosphere of the apartment seemed redolent with suggestions of faded splendour. There was a faint perfume of Russian calf from the many rows of musty volumes which still filled the stately bookcases. The oil paintings which hung upon the walls belonged to a remote period. In a distant corner, four other men were playing bridge, speechless and almost motionless, the white faces of two of them like cameos under the electric light and against the dark walls. There was no sound except the soft patter of the cards and the subdued movements of a servant preparing another bridge table by the side of the three men. Then the door of the room was quietly opened and closed. A man of youthful middle-age, carefully dressed, with a large, clean-shaven face, blue eyes, and fair hair sprinkled with grey, came towards them. He was well set up, almost anxiously ingratiating in manner.

"You see now what Providence has sent," Sir Daniel Harker observed under his breath.

"It is enough to make an atheist of one, this!" the Prince muttered.

"Any bridge?" the newcomer enquired, seating himself at the table and shuffling one of the packs of cards.

The three men rose to their feet with varying degrees of unwillingness.

"Immelan is too good for us," Sir Daniel grumbled. "He always wins."

"I am lucky," the newcomer admitted, "but I may be your partner; in which case, you too will win."

"If you are my partner," the Prince declared, "I shall play for five pounds a hundred. I desire to gamble. London is beginning to weary me."

"Mr. Kingley is a better player, though not so lucky," Immelan acknowledged, with a little bow.

"Never believe it, with all due respect to our young friend here," Sir Daniel replied, as he cut a card. "Kingley plays like a man with brain but without subtlety. In a duel between you two, I would back Immelan every time."

Kingley took his place at the table with a little gesture of resignation. He looked across the table to where Immelan sat displaying the card which he had just cut. The eyes of the two men met. A few seconds of somewhat significant silence followed. Then Immelan gathered up the cards.

"I have the utmost respect for Mr. Kingley as an adversary," he said.

The latter bowed a little ironically.

"May you always preserve that sentiment! To-day, chance seems to have made us partners. Your deal, Mr. Immelan."

"What stakes?" the Prince enquired, settling himself down in his chair.

"They are for you to name," Immelan declared.

The Prince laughed shortly.

"I believe you are as great a gambler at heart as I am," he observed.

"With Mr. Kingley for my partner, and the game one of skill," was the courteous reply, "I do not need to limit my stakes."

A servant crossed the room, bringing a note upon a tray. He presented it to Kingley, who opened and read it through without change of countenance. When he had finished it, however, he laid his cards face downwards upon the table.

"Gentlemen," he said, "I owe you my most profound apologies. I am called away at once on a matter of urgent business."

"But this is most annoying," the Prince declared irritably.

"Here comes my saviour," Kingley remarked, as another man entered the card room. "Henderson will take my place. Glad I haven't to break you up, after all. Henderson, will you play a rubber?"

The newcomer assented. Nigel Kingley made his adieux and crossed the room. Immelan watched him curiously.

"What is our friend Kingley's profession?" he enquired.

"He has no profession," Sir Daniel replied. "He has never come into touch with the sordid needs of these money-grubbing days. He is the nephew and heir of the Earl of Dorminster."

Immelan looked away from the retreating figure.

"Lord Dorminster," he murmured. "The same Lord Dorminster who was in the Government many years ago?"

"He was Foreign Secretary when I was Governor of Jamaica," Sir Daniel answered. "A very brilliant man he was in those days."

Immelan nodded thoughtfully.

"I remember," he said.

Nigel Kingley, on leaving the St. Philip's Club, was driven at once, in the automobile which he found awaiting him, to a large corner house in Belgrave Square, which he entered with the air of an habitué. The waiting major-domo took him at once in charge and piloted him across the hall.

"His lordship is very much occupied, Mr. Nigel," he announced. "He is not seeing any other callers. He left word, however, that you were to be shown in the moment you arrived."

"His lordship is quite well, I hope?"

"Well in health, sir, but worried, and I don't wonder at it," the man replied, speaking with the respectful freedom of an old servant. "I never thought I'd live to see such times as these."

A man in the early sixties, still good-looking, notwithstanding a somewhat worn expression, looked up from his seat at the library table on Kingley's entrance. He nodded, but waited until the door was closed behind the retreating servant before he spoke.

"Good of you to come, Nigel," he said. "Bring your chair up here."

"Bad news?" the newcomer enquired.

"Damnable!"

There was a brief silence, during which Nigel, knowing his uncle's humours, leaned back in his chair and waited. Upon the table was a little pile of closely written manuscript, and by their side several black-bound code books, upon which the "F.O.Private" still remained, though almost obliterated with time. Lord Dorminster's occupation was apparent. He was decoding a message of unusual length. Presently he turned away from the table, however, and faced his nephew. His hands travelled to his waistcoat pocket. He drew out a cigarette from a thin gold case, lit it and began to smoke. Then he crossed his legs and leaned a little farther back in his chair.

"Nigel," he said, "we are living in strange times."

"No one denies that, sir," was the grave assent.

Lord Dorminster glanced at the calendar which stood upon the desk.

"To-day," he continued, "is the twenty-third day of March, nineteen hundred and thirty-four. Fifteen years ago that terrible Peace Treaty was signed. Since then you know what the history of our country has been. I am not blowing my own trumpet when I say that nearly every man with true political insight has been cast adrift. At the present moment the country is in the hands of a body of highly respectable and well-meaning men who, as a parish council, might conduct the affairs of Dorminster Town with unqualified success. As statesmen they do not exist. It seems to me, Nigel, that you and I are going to see in reality that spectre which terrified the world twenty years ago. We are going to see the breaking up of a mighty empire."

"Tell me what has happened or is going to happen," Nigel begged.

"Well, for one thing," his uncle replied, "the Emperor of the East is preparing for a visit to Europe. He will be here probably next month. You know whom I mean, of course?"

"Prince Shan!" Nigel exclaimed.

"Prince Shan of China," Lord Dorminster assented. "His coming links up many things which had been puzzling me. I tell you, Nigel, what happens during Prince Shan's visit will probably decide the destinies of this country, and yet I wouldn't mind betting you a thousand to one that there isn't a single official of the Government who has the slightest idea as to why he is coming, or that he is coming at all."

"Do you know?" Nigel asked.

"I can only surmise. Let us leave Prince Shan for the moment, Nigel. Now listen. You go about a great deal. What do people say about me—honestly, I mean? Speak with your face to the light."

"They call you a faddist and a scaremonger," Nigel confessed, "yet there are one or two, especially at the St. Philip's Club, diplomatists and ambassadors whose place in the world has passed away, who think and believe differently. You know, sir, that I am amongst them."

Lord Dorminster nodded kindly.

"Well," he said, "I fancy I am about to prove myself. Seven years ago, it was," he went on reminiscently, "when the new National Party came into supreme power. You know one of their first battle cries—'Down with all secret treaties! Down with all secret diplomacy! Let nothing exist but an honest commercial understanding between the different countries of the world!' How Germany and Russia howled with joy! In place of an English statesman with his country's broad interests at heart, we have in Berlin and Petrograd half a dozen representatives of the great industries, whose object, in their own words, is, I believe, to develop friendly commercialism and a feeling of brotherhood between the nations. Not only our ambassadors but our secret service were swept clean out of existence. I remember going to Broadley, the day he was appointed Foreign Minister, and I asked him a simple question. I asked him whether he did not consider it his duty to keep his finger upon the pulses of the other great nations, however friendly they might seem, to keep himself assured that all these expressions of good will were honourable, and that in the heart of the German nation that great craving for revenge which is the natural heritage of the present generation had really become dissipated. Broadley smiled at me. 'Lord Dorminster,' he said, 'the chief cause of wars in the past has been suspicion. We look upon espionage as a disgraceful practice. It is the people of Germany with whom we are in touch now, not a military oligarchy, and the people of Germany no more desire war than we do. Besides, there is the League of Nations.' Those were Broadley's views then, and they are his views to-day. You know what I did?"

Nigel assented cautiously.

"I suppose it is an open secret amongst a few of us," he observed. "You have been running an unofficial secret service of your own."

"Precisely! I have had a few agents at work for over a year, and when I have finished decoding this last dispatch, I shall have evidence which will prove beyond a doubt that we are on the threshold of terrible events. The worst of it is—well, we have been found out."

"What do you mean?" Nigel asked quickly.

His uncle's sensitive lips quivered.

"You knew Sidwell?"

"Quite well."

"Sidwell was found stabbed to the heart in a café in Petrograd, three weeks ago," Lord Dorminster announced. "An official report of the enquiry into his death informs his relatives that his death was due to a quarrel with some Russian sailors over one of the women of the quarter where he was found."

"Horrible!" Nigel muttered.

"Sidwell was one of those unnatural people, as you know," Lord Dorminster went on, "who never touched wine or spirits and who hated women. To continue. Atcheson was a friend of yours, wasn't he?"

"Of course! He was at Eton with me. It was I who first brought him here to dine. Don't tell me that anything has happened to Jim Atcheson!"

"This dispatch is from him," Lord Dorminster replied, indicating the pile of manuscript upon the table,—"a dispatch which came into my hands in a most marvellous fashion. He died last week in a nursing home in—well, let us say a foreign capital. The professor in charge of the hospital sends a long report as to the unhappy disease from which he suffered. As a matter of fact, he was poisoned."

Nigel Kingley had been a soldier in his youth and he was a brave man. Nevertheless, the horror of these things struck a cold chill to his heart. He seemed suddenly to be looking into the faces of spectres, to hear the birth of the winds of destruction.

"That is all I have to say to you for the moment," his uncle concluded gravely. "In an hour I shall have finished decoding this dispatch, and I propose then to take you into my entire confidence. In the meantime, I want you to go and talk for a few minutes to the cleverest woman in England, the woman who, in the face of a whole army of policemen and detectives, crossed the North Sea yesterday afternoon with this in her pocket."

"You don't mean Maggie?" Nigel exclaimed eagerly.

His uncle nodded.

"You will find her in the boudoir," he said. "I told her that you were coming. In an hour's time, return here."

Lord Dorminster rose to his feet as his nephew turned to depart. He laid his hand upon the latter's shoulder, and Nigel always remembered the grave kindliness of his tone and expression.

"Nigel," he sighed, "I am afraid I shall be putting upon your shoulders a terrible burden, but there is no one else to whom I can turn."

"There is no one else to whom you ought to turn, sir," the young man replied simply. "I shall be back in an hour."

II

L ady Maggie Trent, a stepdaughter of the Earl of Dorminster, was one of those young women who had baffled description for some years before she had commenced to take life seriously. She was neither fair nor dark, petite nor tall. No one could ever have called her nondescript, or have extolled any particular grace of form or feature. Her complexion had defied the ravages of sun and wind and that moderate indulgence in cigarettes and cocktails which the youth of her day affected. Her nose was inclined to be retroussé, her mouth tender but impudent, her grey eyes mostly veiled in expression but capable of wonderful changes. She was curled up in a chair when Nigel entered, immersed in a fashion paper. She held out her left hand, which he raised to his lips.

"Well, Nigel, dear," she exclaimed, "what do you think of my new profession?"

"I hate it," he answered frankly.

She sighed and laid down the fashion paper resignedly.

"You always did object to a woman doing anything in the least useful. Do you realise that if anything in the world can save this stupid old country, I have done it?"

"I realise that you've been running hideous risks," he replied.

She looked at him petulantly.

"What of it?" she demanded. "We all run risks when we do anything worth while."

"Not quite the sort that you have been facing."

She smiled thoughtfully.

"Do you know exactly where I have been?" she asked.

"No idea," he confessed. "What my uncle has just told me was a complete revelation, so far as I was concerned. I believed, with the rest of the world, what the newspapers announced—that you were visiting Japan and China, and afterwards the South Sea Islands, with the Wendercombes."

She smiled.

"Dad wanted to tell you," she said, "but it was I who made him promise not to. I was afraid you would be disagreeable about it. We arranged it all with the Wendercombes, but as a matter of fact I did not even start with them. For the last eight months, I have been living part of the time in Berlin and part of the time in a country house near the Black Forest."

"Alone?"

"Not a bit of it! I have been governess to the two daughters of Herr Essendorf."

"Essendorf, the President of the German Republic?"

Lady Maggie nodded.

"He isn't a bit like his pictures. He is a huge fat man and he eats a great deal too much. Oh, the horror of those meals!" she added, with a little shudder. "Think of me, dear Nigel, who never eat more than an omelette and some fruit for luncheon, compelled to sit down every day to a *mittagessen*! I wonder I have any digestion left at all."

"Do you mean that you were there under your own name?" he asked incredulously.

She shook her head.

"I secured some perfectly good testimonials before I left," she said. "They referred to a Miss Brown, the daughter of Prebendary Brown. I was Miss Brown."

"Great Heavens!" Nigel muttered under his breath. "You heard about Atcheson?"

She nodded.

"Poor fellow, they got him all right. You talk about thrills, Nigel," she went on. "Do you know that the last night before I left for my vacation, I actually heard that fat old Essendorf chuckling with his wife about how his clever police had laid an English spy by the heels, and telling her, also, of the papers which they had discovered and handed over. All the time the real dispatch, written by Atcheson when he was dying, was sewn into my corsets. How's that for an exciting situation?"

"It's a man's job, anyhow," Nigel declared.

She shrugged her shoulders and abandoned the personal side of the subject.

"Have you been in Germany lately, Nigel?" she enquired.

"Not for many years," he answered.

She stretched herself out upon the couch and lit a cigarette.

"The Germany of before the war of course I can't remember," she said pensively. "I imagine, however, that there was a sort of instinctive jealous dislike towards England and everything English, simply because England had had a long start in colonisation, commerce and all the rest of it. But the feeling in Germany now, although it is marvellously hidden, is something perfectly amazing. It absolutely vibrates wherever you go. The silence makes it all the more menacing. Soon after I got to Berlin, I bought a copy of the Treaty of Peace and read it. Nigel, was it necessary to have been so bitterly cruel to a beaten enemy?"

"Logically it would seem not," Nigel admitted. "Actually, we cannot put ourselves back into the spirit of those days. You must remember that it was an unprovoked war, a war engineered by Germany for the sheer purposes of aggression. That is why a punitive spirit entered into our subsequent negotiations."

She nodded.

"I expect history will tell us some day," she continued, "that we needed a great statesman of the Beaconsfield type at the Peace table. However, that is all ended. They sowed the seed at Versailles, and I think we are going to reap the harvest."

"After all," Nigel observed thoughtfully, "it is very difficult to see what practical interference there could be with the peace of the world. I can very well believe that the spirit is there, but when it comes to hard facts—well, what can they do? England can never be invaded. The war of 1914 proved that. Besides, Germany now has a representative on the League of Nations. She is bound to toe the line with the rest."

"It is not in Germany alone that we are disliked," Maggie reminded him. "We seem somehow or other to have found our way into the bad books of every country in Europe. Clumsy statesmanship is it, or what?"

"I should attribute it," Nigel replied, "to the passing of our old school of ambassadors. After all, ambassadors are born, not made, and they should be—they very often were—men of rare tact and perceptions. We have no one now to inform us of the prejudices and humours of the nations. We often offend quite unwittingly, and we miss many opportunities of a *rapprochement*. It is trade, trade, trade and nothing else, the whole of the time, and the men whom we sent to the different Courts to further our commercial interests are not the type to keep us informed of the more subtle and intricate matters which sometimes need adjustment between two countries."

"That may be the explanation of all the bad feeling," Maggie admitted, "and you may be right when you say that any practical move against us is almost impossible. Dad doesn't think so, you know. He is terribly exercised about the coming of Prince Shan."

"I must get him to talk to me," Nigel said. "As a matter of fact, I don't think that we need fear Asiatic intervention over here. Prince Shan is too great a diplomatist to risk his country's new prosperity."

"Prince Shan," Maggie declared, "is the one man in the world I am longing to meet. He was at Oxford with you, wasn't he, Nigel?"

"For one year only. He went from there to Harvard."

"Tell me what he was like," she begged.

"I have only a hazy recollection of him," Nigel confessed. "He was a most brilliant scholar and a fine horseman. I can't remember whether he did anything at games."

"Good-looking?"

"Extraordinarily so. He was very reserved, though, and even in those days he was far more exclusive than our own royal princes. We all thought him clever, but no one dreamed that he would become Asia's great man. I'll tell you all that I can remember about him another time, Maggie. I'm rather curious about that report of Atcheson's. Have you any idea what it is about?"

She shook her head.

"None at all. It is in the old Foreign Office cipher and it looks like gibberish. I only know that the first few lines he transcribed gave dad the jumps."

"I wonder if he has finished it by now."

"He'll send for you when he has. How do you think I am looking, Nigel?"

"Wonderful," he answered, rising to his feet and standing with his elbow upon the mantelpiece, gazing down at her. "But then you *are* wonderful, aren't you, Maggie? You know I always thought so."

She picked up a mirror from the little bag by her side and scrutinized her features.

"It can't be my face," she decided, turning towards him with a smile. "I must have charm."

"Your face is adorable," he declared.

"Are you going to flirt with me?" she asked, with a faint smile at the corners of her lips. "You always do it so well and so convincingly. And I hate foreigners. They are terribly in earnest but there is no finesse about them. You may kiss me just once, please, Nigel, the way I like."

He held her for a moment in his arms, tenderly, but with a reserve to which she was accustomed from him. Presently she thrust him away. Her own colour had risen a little.

"Delightful," she murmured. "Think of the wasted months! No one has kissed me, Nigel, since we said good-bye."

"Have you made up your mind to marry me yet?" he asked.

"My dear," she answered, patting his hand, "do restrain your ardour. Do you really want to marry me?"

"Of course I do!"

"You don't love me."

"I am awfully fond of you," he assured her, "and I don't love any one else."

She shook her head.

"It isn't enough, Nigel," she declared, "and, strange to say, it's exactly how I feel about you."

"I don't see why it shouldn't be enough," he argued. "Perhaps we have too much common sense for these violent feelings."

"It may be that," she admitted doubtfully. "On the other hand, don't let's run any risk. I should hate to find an affinity, and all that sort of thing, after marriage—divorce in these days is such shocking bad form. Besides, honestly, Nigel, I don't feel frivolous enough to think about marriage just now. I have the feeling that even while the clock is ticking we are moving on to terrible things. I can't tell you quite what it is. I carried my life in my hands during those last few days abroad. I dare say this is the reaction."

He smiled reassuringly.

"After all, you are safe at home now, dear," he reminded her, "and I really am very fond of you, Maggie."

"And I'm quite absurdly fond of you, Nigel," she acknowledged. "It makes me feel quite uncomfortable when I reflect that I shall probably have to order you to make love to some one else before the week is out."

"I shall do nothing of the sort," he declared firmly. "I am not good at that sort of thing. And who is she, anyhow?"

They were interrupted by a sudden knock at the door—not the discreet tap of a well-bred domestic, but a flurried, almost an imperative summons. Before either of them could reply, the door was opened and Brookes, the elderly butler, presented himself upon the threshold. Even before he spoke, it was clear that he brought alarming news.

"Will you step down to the library at once, sir?" he begged, addressing Nigel.

"What is the matter, Brookes?" Maggie demanded anxiously.

"I fear that his lordship is not well," the man replied.

They all hurried out together. Brookes was evidently terribly perturbed and went on talking half to himself without heeding their questions.

"I thought at first that his lordship must have fainted," he said. "I heard a queer noise, and when I went in, he had fallen forward across the table. Parkins has rung for Doctor Wilcox."

"What sort of a noise?" Nigel asked.

"It sounded like a shot," the man faltered.

They entered the library, Nigel leading the way. Lord Dorminster was lying very much as Brookes had described him, but there was something altogether unnatural in the collapse of his head and shoulders and his motionless body. Nigel spoke to him, touched him gently, raised him at last into a sitting position. Something on which his right hand seemed to have been resting clattered on to the carpet. Nigel turned around and waved Maggie back.

"Don't come," he begged.

"Is it a stroke?" she faltered.

"I am afraid that he is dead," Nigel answered simply.

They went out into the hall and waited there in shocked silence until the doctor arrived. The latter's examination lasted only a few seconds. Then he pointed to the telephone.

"This is very terrible," he said. "I am afraid you had better ring up Scotland Yard, Mr. Kingley. Lord Dorminster appears either to have shot himself, as seems most probable," he added, glancing at the revolver upon the carpet, "or to have been murdered."

"It is incredible!" Nigel exclaimed. "He was the sanest possible man, and the happiest, and he hadn't an enemy in the world."

The physician pointed downwards to the revolver. Then he unfastened once more the dead man's waistcoat, opened his shirt and indicated a small blue mark just over his heart.

"That is how he died," he said. "It must have been instantaneous."

Time seemed to beat out its course in leaden seconds whilst they waited for the superintendent from Scotland Yard. Nigel at first stood still for some moments. From outside came the cheerful but muffled roar of the London streets, the hooting of motor horns, the rumbling of wheels, the measured footfall of the passing multitude. A boy went by, whistling; another passed, calling hoarsely the news from the afternoon papers. A muffin man rang his bell, a small boy clattered his stick against the area bailing. The whole world marched on, unmoved and unnoticing. In this sombre apartment alone tragedy reigned in sinister silence. On the sofa, Lord Dorminster, who only half an hour ago had seemed to be in the prime of life and health, lay dead.

Nigel moved towards the writing-table and stood looking at it in wonder. The code book still remained, but there was not the slightest sign of any manuscript or paper of any sort. He even searched the drawers of the desk without result. Every trace of Atcheson's dispatch and Lord Dorminster's transcription of it had disappeared!

III

On a certain day some weeks after the adjourned inquest and funeral of Lord Dorminster, Nigel obtained a long-sought-for interview with the Right Honourable Mervin Brown, who had started life as a factory inspector and was now Prime Minister of England. The great man received his visitor with an air of good-natured tolerance.

"Heard of you from Scotland Yard, haven't I, Lord Dorminster?" he said, as he waved him to a seat. "I gather that you disagreed very strongly with the open verdict which was returned at the inquest upon your uncle?"

"The verdict was absolutely at variance with the facts," Nigel declared. "My uncle was murdered, and a secret report of certain doings on the continent, which he was decoding at the time, was stolen."

"The medical evidence scarcely bears out your statement," Mr. Mervin Brown pointed out dryly, "nor have the police been able to discover how any one could have obtained access to the room, or left it, without leaving some trace of their visit behind. Further, there are no indications of a robbery having been attempted."

"I happen to know more than any one else about this matter," Nigel urged,—"more, even, than I thought it advisable to mention at the inquest—and I beg you to listen to me, Mr. Mervin Brown. I know that you considered my uncle to be in some respects a crank, because he was far-seeing enough to understand that under the seeming tranquillity abroad there is a universal and deep-seated hatred of this country."

"I look upon that statement as misleading and untrue," the Minister declared. "Your late uncle belonged to that mischievous section of foreign politicians who believed in secret treaties and secret service, and who fostered a state of nervous unrest between countries otherwise disposed to be friendly. We have turned over a new leaf, Lord Dorminster. Our efforts are all directed towards developing an international spirit of friendliness and trust."

"Utopian but very short-sighted," Nigel commented. "If my uncle had lived to finish decoding the report upon which he was engaged, I could have offered you proof not only of the existence of the spirit I speak of, but of certain practical schemes inimical to this country."

"The papers you speak of have disappeared," Mr. Mervin Brown observed, with a smile.

"They were taken away by the person who murdered my uncle," Nigel insisted.

The Right Honourable gentleman nodded.

"Well, you know my views about the affair," he said. "I may add that they are confirmed by the police. I am in no way prejudiced, however, and am willing to listen to anything you may have to say which will not take you more than a quarter of an hour," he added, glancing at the clock upon his table.

"Here goes, then," Nigel began. "My uncle was a statesman of the old school who had no faith in the Utopian programme of the present Government of this country. When you abandoned any pretence of a continental secret service, he at his own expense instituted a small one of his own. He sent two men out to Germany and one to Russia. The one sent to Russia was the man Sidwell, whose murder in a Petrograd café you may have read of. Of the two sent to Germany, one has disappeared, and the other died in hospital, without a doubt poisoned, a few days after he had sent the report to England which was stolen from my uncle's desk. That report was brought over by Lady Maggie Trent, Lord Dorminster's stepdaughter, who was really the brains of the enterprise and under another name was acting as governess to the children of Herr Essendorf, President of the German Republic. Half an hour before his death, my uncle was decoding this dispatch in his library. I saw him doing it, and I saw the dispatch itself. He told me that so far as he had gone already, it was full of information of the gravest import; that a definite scheme was already being formulated against this country by an absolutely unique and dangerous combination of enemies."

"Those enemies being?"

Nigel shook his head.

"That I can only surmise," he replied. "My uncle had only commenced to decode the dispatch when I last saw him."

"Then I gather, Lord Dorminster," the Minister said, "that you connect your uncle's death directly with the supposed theft of this document?"

"Absolutely!"

"And the conclusion you arrive at, then?"

"Is an absolutely logical one," Nigel declared firmly. "I assert that other countries are not falling into line with our lamentable abnegation of all secret service defence, and that, in plain words, my uncle was murdered by an agent of one of these countries, in order that the dispatch which had come into his hands should not be decoded and passed on to your Government."

The Right Honourable gentleman smiled slightly. He was a man of some natural politeness, but he found it hard to altogether conceal his incredulity.

"Well, Lord Dorminster," he promised, "I will consider all that you have said. Is there anything more I can do for you?"

"Yes!" Nigel replied boldly. "Induce the Cabinet to reëstablish our Intelligence Department and secret service, even on a lesser scale, and don't rest until you have discovered exactly what it is they are plotting against us somewhere on the continent."

"To carry out your suggestions, Lord Dorminster," the Minister pointed out, "would be to be guilty of an infringement of the spirit of the League of Nations, the existence of which body is, we believe, a practical assurance of our safety."

Nigel rose to his feet.

"As man to man, sir," he said, "I see you don't believe a word of what I have been telling you."

"As man to man," the other admitted pleasantly, as he touched the bell, "I think you have been deceived."

NIGEL, EVEN AS A PROPHET of woe, was a very human person and withal a philosopher. He strolled along Piccadilly and turned into Bond Street, thoroughly enjoying one of the first spring days of the season. Flower sellers were busy at every corner; the sky was blue, with tiny flecks of white clouds, there was even some dust stirred by the little puffs of west wind. He exchanged greetings with a few acquaintances, lingered here and there before the shop windows, and presently developed a fit of contemplation engendered by the thoughts which were all the time at the back of his mind. Bond Street was crowded with vehicles of all sorts, from wonderfully upholstered automobiles to the resuscitated victoria. The shop windows were laden with the treasures of the world, buyers were plentiful, promenaders multitudinous. Every one seemed to be cheerful but a little engrossed in the concrete act of living. Nigel almost ran into Prince Karschoff, at the corner of Grafton Street.

"Dreaming, my friend?" the latter asked quietly, as he laid his hand upon Nigel's shoulder.

"Guilty," Nigel confessed. "You are an observant man, Prince. Tell me whether anything strikes you about the Bond Street of to-day, compared with the Bond Street of, say, ten years ago?"

The Russian glanced around him curiously. He himself was a somewhat unusual figure in his distinctively cut morning coat, his carefully tied cravat, his silk hat, black and white check trousers and faultless white spats.

"A certain decline of elegance," he murmured. "And is it my fancy or has this country become a trifle Americanised as regards the headgear of its men?"

Nigel smiled.

"I believe our thoughts are moving in the same groove," he said. "To me there seems to be a different class of people here, as though the denizens of West Kensington, suddenly enriched, had come to spend their money in new quarters. Not only that, but there is a difference in the wares set out in the shops, an absence of taste, if you can understand what I mean, as though the shopkeepers themselves understood that they were catering for a new class of people."

"It is the triumph of your *bourgeoisie*," the Russian declared. "Your aristocrat is no longer able to survive. *Noblesse oblige* has no significance to the shopman. He wants the fat cheques, and he caters for the people who can write them. Let us pursue our reflections a little farther and in a different direction, my friend," he added, glancing at his watch. "Lunch with me at the Ritz, and we will see whether the cookery, too, has been adapted to the new tastes."

Nigel hesitated for a moment, a somewhat curious hesitation which he many times afterwards remembered.

"I am not very keen on restaurants for a week or two," he said doubtfully. "Besides, I had half promised to be at the club."

"Not to-day," Karschoff insisted. "To-day let us listen to the call of the world. Woman is at her loveliest in the spring. The Ritz Restaurant will look like a bouquet of flowers. Perhaps 'One for you and one for me.' At any rate, one is sure of an omelette one can eat."

The two men turned together towards Piccadilly.

IV

Luncheon at the Ritz was an almost unexpectedly pleasant meal. The two men sat at a table near the door and exchanged greetings with many acquaintances. Karschoff, who was in an unusually loquacious frame of mind, pointed out many of the habitués of the place to his companion.

"I am become a club and restaurant lounger in my old age," he declared, a little bitterly. "Almost a boulevardier. Still, what else is there for a man without a country to do?"

"You know everybody," Nigel replied, without reference to his companion's lament. "Tell me who the woman is who has just entered?"

Karschoff glanced in the direction indicated, and for a moment his somewhat saturnine expression changed. A smile played upon his lips, his eyes seemed to rest upon the figure of the girl half turned away from them with interest, almost with pleasure. She was of an unusual type, tall and dark, dressed in black with the simplicity of a nun, with only a little gleam of white at her throat. Her hair—so much of it as showed under her flower-garlanded hat—was as black as jet, and yet, where she stood in the full glare of the sunlight, the burnish of it was almost wine-coloured. Her cheeks were pale, her expression thoughtful. Her eyes, rather heavily lidded, were a deep shade of violet. Her mouth was unexpectedly soft and red.

"Ah, my friend, no wonder you ask!" Karschoff declared with enthusiasm. "That is a woman whom you must know."

"Tell me her name," Nigel persisted with growing impatience.

"Her name," Karschoff replied, "is Naida Karetsky. She is the daughter of the man who will probably be the next President of the Russian Republic. You see, I can speak those words without a tremor. Her father at present represents the shipping interests of Russia and England. He is one of the authorised consuls."

"Is he of the party?"

Karschoff scrutinised the approaching figures through his eyeglass and nodded.

"Her father is the dark, broad-shouldered man with the square beard," he indicated. "Immelan, as you can see, is the third. They are coming this way. We will speak of them afterwards."

Naida, with her father and Oscar Immelan, left some acquaintances with whom they had been talking and, preceded by a *maître d'hôtel*, moved in the direction of the two men. The girl recognised the Prince with a charming little bow and was on the point of passing on when she appeared to notice his companion. For a moment she hesitated. The Prince, anticipating her desire to speak, rose at once to his feet.

"Mademoiselle," he said, bending over her hand, "welcome back to England! You bring with you the first sunshine we have seen for many days."

"Are you being meteorological or complimentary?" she asked, smiling. "Will you present your companion? I have heard of Mr. Kingley."

"With the utmost pleasure," the Prince replied. "Mr. Kingley, through the unfortunate death of a relative, is now the Earl of Dorminster—Mademoiselle Karetsky."

Nigel, as he made his bow, was conscious of an expression of something more than ordinary curiosity in the face of the girl who had herself aroused his interest.

"You are the son, then," she enquired, "of Lord Dorminster who died about a month ago?"

"His nephew," Nigel explained. "My uncle was unfortunately childless."

"I met your uncle once in Paris," she said. "It will give me great pleasure to make your better acquaintance. Will you and my dear friend here," she added, turning to the Prince, "take coffee with us afterwards? I shall then introduce you to my father. Oscar Immelan you both know, of course."

They murmured their delighted assent, and she passed on. Nigel watched her until she took her place at the table.

"Surely that girl is well-born?" he observed. "I have never seen a more delightful carriage."

"You are right," Karschoff told him. "Karetsky is a well-to-do man of commerce, but her mother was a Baroness Kolchekoff, a distant relative of my own. The Kolchekoffs lived on their estates, and as a matter of fact we never met. Naida has gone over to the people, though, body and soul."

"She is extraordinarily beautiful," Nigel remarked.

His companion was swinging his eyeglass back and forth by its cord.

"Many men have thought so," he replied. "For myself, there is antagonism in my blood against her. I wonder whether I have done well or ill in making you two acquainted."

Nigel felt a sudden desire to break through a certain seriousness which had come over his own thoughts and which was reflected in the other's tone. He shrugged his shoulders slightly and filled his glass with wine.

"Every man in the world is the better," he propounded, "for adding to the circle of his acquaintants a beautiful woman."

"Sententious and a trifle inaccurate," the Prince objected, with a sudden flash of his white teeth. "The beauty which is not for him has been many a man's undoing. But seriously, my quarrel with Naida is one of prejudice only. She is the confidante and the inspiration of Matinsky, and though one realises, of course, that so long as there is a Russian Republic there must be a Russian President, I suppose I should scarcely be human if I did not hate him."

"Surely," Nigel queried, "she must be very much his junior?"

"Matinsky is forty-four," Karschoff said. "Naida is twenty-six or twenty-seven. The disparity of years, you see, is not so great. Matinsky, however, is married to an invalid wife, and concerning Naida I have never heard one word of scandal. But this much is certain. Matinsky has the blandest confidence in her judgment and discretion. She has already been his unofficial ambassador in several capitals of Europe. I am convinced that she is here with a purpose. But enough of my country-people. We came here to be gay. Let us drink another bottle of wine."

The joy of living seemed for a moment to reassert itself in Karschoff's face. His momentary fierceness, reminiscent of his Tartar ancestry, had passed, but it had left a shadow behind.

"At least one should be grateful," he conceded a moment later, "for the distinction such a woman as Naida Karetsky brings into a room like this. Our Bond Street lament finds its proof here. Except for their clothes—so ill-worn, too, most of them—the women here remind one of Blackpool, and their men of Huddersfield. I am inclined to wish that I had taken you to Soho."

Nigel shook his head. His eyes had strayed to a distant corner of the room, where Naida and her two companions were seated.

"We cannot escape anywhere," he declared, "from this overmastering wave of mediocrity. A couple of generations and a little intermarriage may put things right. A Chancellor of the Exchequer with genius, fifteen years ago, might even have prevented it."

"You can claim, at any rate, a bloodless and unapparent revolution," the Prince observed. "You chivied your aristocracy of birth out of existence with yellow papers, your aristocracy of mind with a devastating income tax. This is the class whom you left to gorge,—the war profiteers. I hope that whoever writes the history of these times will see that it is properly illustrated."

In the lounge, they had barely seated themselves before Naida, with her father and Immelan, appeared. The little party at once joined up, and Naida seated herself next to Nigel. She talked very slowly, but her accent amounted to little more than a prolongation of certain syllables, which had the effect of a rather musical drawl. Her father, after the few words of introduction had been spoken, strolled away to speak to some acquaintances, and Immelan and the Prince discussed with measured politeness one of the commonplace subjects of the moment. Naida and her companion became almost isolated.

"I met your uncle once," Naida said, "at a dinner party in Paris. I remember that he attracted me. He represented a class of Englishman of whom I had met very few, the thinking aristocrat with a sense for foreign affairs. It was some years ago, that. He remained outside politics, did he not, until his death?"

"Outside all practical politics," Nigel assented. "He had his interests, though."

She looked at him thoughtfully.

"Have you inherited them?" she asked.

He declined the challenge of her eyes. After all, she belonged to the Russia whose growing strength was the greatest menace to European peace, and whose attitude towards England was entirely uncertain.

"My uncle and I were scarcely intimate," he said. "I was never really in his confidence."

"Not so much so as Lady Maggie Trent? She would be your cousin?"

"It is not a relationship of blood," Nigel replied. "Lady Maggie was the daughter of my uncle's second wife."

"She is very charming," Naida murmured.

"I find her delightful," Nigel agreed.

"She is not only charming, but she has intelligence," Naida continued. "I think that Lord Dorminster was very fond of her, that he trusted her with many of his secrets."

"Had he secrets?" Nigel asked.

She remained for a moment very thoughtful, smoking a thin cigarette through a long holder and watching the little rings of smoke.

"You are right," she said at last. "I find your attitude the only correct one. Did you know that Maggie was a friend of mine, Lord Dorminster?"

"I can very well believe it," he answered, "but I have never heard her speak of you."

"Ah! But she has been away for some months. You have not seen much of her, perhaps, since her return?"

"Very little," he acquiesced. "She only arrived in London just before my uncle's death, and since then I have had to spend some time at Dorminster."

"As a matter of curiosity," Naida enquired, "when do you expect to see her again?"

"This afternoon, I hope," he replied,—"directly I leave here, in fact."

"Then you will give her a little message for me, please?"

"With great pleasure!"

"Tell her from me—mind she understands this, if you please—that she is not to leave England again until we have met."

"Is this a warning?" he asked.

She looked at him searchingly.

"I wonder," she reflected, "how much of you is Lord Dorminster's nephew."

"And I, in my turn," he rejoined, with sudden boldness, "wonder how much of you is Matinsky's envoy."

She began to laugh softly.

"We shall perhaps be friends, Lord Dorminster," she said. "I should like to see more of you."

"You will permit me to call upon you," he begged eagerly.

"Will you come? We are at the Milan Court for a little time. My father is trying to get a house. My sister is coming over to look after him. I am unfortunately only a bird of passage."

"Then I shall not run the risk of missing you," he declared. "I shall call very soon."

Immelan intervened,—grim, suspicious, a little disturbed. For some reason or other, the meeting between these two young people seemed to have made him uneasy.

"Your father has desired me to present his excuses to Lord Dorminster," he announced, "and to escort you back to the Milan. He has been telephoned for from the Consulate."

Naida rose to her feet with some apparent reluctance.

"You will not delay your call too long, Lord Dorminster?" she enjoined, as she gave him her hand. "I shall expect you the first afternoon you are free."

"I shall not delay giving myself the pleasure," he assured her.

She nodded and made her adieux to the Prince. The two men stood together and watched her depart with her companion.

"Really, one gains much through being an onlooker," the Prince reflected. "There go the spirit of Russia and the spirit of Germany. You dabble in these things, my friend Dorminster. Can you guess what they are met for—for whom they wait?"

"I might guess," Nigel replied, "but I would rather be told."

"They wait for the master spirit," Karschoff declared, taking his arm. "They wait for the great Prince Shan."

V

Nigel and Maggie had tea together in the little room which the latter had used as a boudoir. They were discussing the question of her future residence there.

"I am afraid," he declared, "that you will have to marry me."

"It would have its advantages," she admitted thoughtfully. "I am really so fond of you, Nigel. I should be married at St. Mary Abbot's, Kensington, and have the Annersley children for bridesmaids. Don't you think I should look sweet in old gold and orange blossoms?"

"Don't tantalise me," he begged.

"We really must decide upon something," she insisted. "I hate giving up my rooms here, I should hate having my worthy aunt as resident duenna, and I suppose it would be gloriously improper for us two to go on living here if I didn't. Are you quite sure that you love me, Nigel?"

"I am not quite so sure as I was this morning," he confessed, holding out his cup for some more tea. "I met a perfectly adorable girl to-day at luncheon at the Ritz. Such eyes, Maggie, and the slimmest, most wonderful figure you ever saw!"

"Who was the cat?" Maggie enquired with asperity.

"She is Russian. Her name is Naida Karetsky. Karschoff introduced me."

Maggie was suddenly serious. There was just a trace of the one expression he had never before seen in her face—fear—lurking in her eyes, even asserting itself in her tone.

"Naida Karetsky?" she repeated. "Tell me exactly how you met her?"

"She was lunching with her father and Oscar Immelan. She stopped to speak to Karschoff and asked him to present me. Afterwards, she invited us to take coffee in the lounge."

"She went out of her way to make your acquaintance, then?"

"Yes, I suppose she did."

"You know who she is?"

"The daughter of one of the Russian Consuls over here, I understood."

"She is more than that," Maggie declared nervously. "She is the inspiration of the President himself. She is the most vital force in Russian politics. She is the woman whom I wanted you to know, to whom I told you that I wished you to pay attentions. And now that you know her, I am afraid."

"Where did you meet her?" he asked curiously.

"We were at school together in Paris. She was two years older than I, but she stayed there until she was twenty. Afterwards we met in Florence."

Nigel was greatly interested.

"Somehow or other, nothing that you can tell me about her surprises me," he admitted. "She has the air of counting for great things in the world. She is very beautiful, too."

"She is beautiful enough," Maggie replied, "to have turned the head of the great Paul Matinsky himself. They say that he would give his soul to be free to marry her. As it is, she is the uncrowned Tsarina of Russia."

Nigel frowned slightly.

"Isn't that going rather a long way?" he objected.

"Not when one remembers what manner of a man Matinsky is," Maggie replied. "He may have his faults, but he is an absolute idealist so far as regards his private life. There has never been a word of scandal concerning him and Naida, nor will there ever be. But in his eyes, Naida has that most wonderful gift of all,—she has vision. He once told a man with whom I spoke in Berlin that Naida was the one person in the world to whom a mistake was impossible. Nigel, did she give you any idea at all what she was over here for?"

"Not as yet," he replied, "but she has asked me to go and see her."

"Did she seem interested in you personally, or was it because your name is Dorminster?"

Nigel sighed.

"I hoped it was a personal interest, but I cannot tell. She asked me whether I had inherited my uncle's hobby."

"What did you tell her?" she asked eagerly.

"Very little. She seemed sympathetic, but after all she is in the enemy camp. She and Immelan seemed on particularly good terms."

"Yet I don't believe that she is committed as yet," Maggie declared. "She always used to speak so affectionately of England. Nigel, do you think that I have vision?"

"I am sure that you have," he answered.

"Very well, then, I will tell you what I see," she continued. "I see Naida Karetsky for Russia, Oscar Immelan for Germany, Austria and Sweden, and Prince Shan for Asia—here—meeting in London— within the next week or ten days, to take counsel together to decide whether the things which are being plotted against us to-day shall be or shall not be. Of Immelan we have no hope. He conceals it cleverly enough, but he hates England with all the fervour of a zealot. Naida is unconvinced. She is to be won. And Prince Shan—"

"Well, what about him?" Nigel demanded, a little carried away by Maggie's earnestness.

She shook her head.

"I don't know," she confessed. "If the stories one hears about him are true, no man nor any woman could ever influence him. At least, though, one could watch and hope."

"Prince Shan is supposed to be coming to Paris, not to London," Nigel remarked.

"If he goes to Paris," Maggie said, "Naida and Immelan will go. So shall we. If he comes here, it will be easier. Tell me, Nigel, did you see the Prime Minister?"

"I saw him," Nigel replied, "but without the slightest result. He is clearly of the opinion that the open verdict was a merciful one. In other words, he believes that it was a case of suicide."

"How wicked!" Maggie exclaimed.

"I suppose it is trying the ordinary Britisher a little high," Nigel remarked, "to ask him to believe that he was murdered in cold blood, here in the heart of London, by the secret service agent of a foreign Power. The strangest part of it all is that it is true. To think that those few pages of manuscript would have told us exactly what we have to fear! Why, I actually had them in my hand."

"And I in my corsets!" Maggie groaned.

They were both silent for a moment. Then Nigel moved towards the door and opened it.

"Come downstairs into the library, will you, Maggie?" he begged. "Let us go in for a little reconstruction."

They found Brookes in the hall and took him with them. The blinds in the room had never been raised, and there was still that nameless atmosphere which lingers for long in an apartment which has become associated with tragedy. Instinctively they all moved quietly and spoke in hushed voices. Nigel sat in the chair where his uncle had been found dead and made a mental effort to reconstruct the events which must have immediately preceded the tragedy.

"I know that this was all thrashed out at the inquest, Brookes," he said, "but I want you to tell me once more. You see how far it is from this table to the door. My uncle must have had abundant warning of any one approaching. Was there no other way by which any one could have entered the room?"

"There was, your lordship," the man replied, "and I have regretted several times since that I did not mention it at the inquest. The cleaners were here on the morning of that day, and the window at the farther end of the room was unfastened—I even believe that it was open."

Nigel rose and examined the window in question. It was almost flush with the ground, and although there were iron railings separating it from the street, a little gate opening from the area entrance made ingress not only possible but easy. Nigel returned to his chair.

"I can't understand this not having been mentioned at the inquest, Brookes," he said.

"I was waiting for the question to be asked, your lordship. It was perfectly clear to every one there, if your lordship will excuse my saying so, that both the coroner and the police seemed to have made up their minds that it was a case of suicide."

Nigel nodded.

"I had the same idea with reference to the coroner, at any rate, Brookes," he said. "So long as the verdict was returned in the form it was, I am not sure that it was not better so."

He dismissed the man with a little nod and sat turning over the code books which still stood upon the table.

"You and I, at any rate, Maggie, know the truth," he said, "and so long as we can get no help from the proper quarters, I think that we should do better to let the matter remain as it is. We don't want to direct people's attention to us. We want to lull suspicion so far as we can, to be free to watch the three."

The telephone bell rang, and as Nigel moved his arm to take off the receiver, he knocked over one of the black, morocco-bound code books, A sheet of paper with a few words upon it came fluttering to the ground. Maggie picked it up, glanced at it carelessly at first and then with interest.

"Nigel," she exclaimed, "you see whose handwriting this is? Could it be part of the decoded dispatch?"

The telephone enquiry had been unimportant. Nigel pushed the instrument away. They both looked eagerly at the page of manuscript paper. It was numbered "8" at the top, and the few words written upon it in Lord Dorminster's writing were obviously the continuation of a paragraph:

The name of the middle one, then, of the three secret cities, into which at all costs some one must find his way, is Kroten, and the telephone number which is all the clue I have been able to get, up to the present, to the London end of the affair, is Mayfair 146.

"This is just where he got to in the decoding!" Nigel declared. "I wonder whether it's any use looking for the rest."

They searched through every page of the heavy code books in vain. Then they returned to their study of the single page. Nigel dragged down an atlas and studied it.

"Kroten," he muttered. "Here it is,—a small place about six hundred miles from Petrograd, apparently the centre of a barren, swampy district, population thirty thousand, birth rate declining, industries nil. Cheerful sort of spot it seems!"

"I have more luck than you!" Maggie cried, her finger tracing out a line in the open telephone book. "Look!"

Nigel glanced over her shoulder and read the entry to which she was pointing:

"Immelan Oscar, 13 Clarges Street, W. Mayfair 146."

VI

Nigel played golf at Ranelagh, on the following Sunday morning, with Jere Chalmers, a young American in the Diplomatic Service, who had just arrived in London and brought a letter of introduction to him. They had a pleasant game and strolled off from the eighteenth green to the dressing rooms on the best of terms with each other.

"Say, Dorminster," his young companion enjoined, "let's get through this fixing-up business quickly. I've had a kind of feeling for a cocktail, these last four holes, which I can't exactly put into words. Besides, I want to have a word or two with you before the others come down."

"I shan't be a minute," Nigel promised. "I'm going to change into flannels after lunch—that is, if you don't mind playing a set or two at tennis. My cousin-in-law Maggie Trent, whom you'll meet at luncheon, is rather keen, and she doesn't care about golf."

"I'm game for anything," the other agreed, lifting his head spluttering from the basin. "Gee, that's good! Get a move on, there's a good fellow. I have a fancy for just five minutes with you out on the lawn, with the ice chinking in our glasses."

Nigel finished smoothing his hair, and the two men strolled through the hall, gave an order to a red-coated attendant, and found a secluded table under a marvellous tree in the gardens on the other side. Chalmers had become a little thoughtful.

"Dorminster," he declared, "yours is a wonderful country."

"Just how is it appealing to you at the moment?" Nigel enquired.

"I'll try and tell you," was the meditative reply. "It's your extraordinary insouciance. It seems to me, as a budding diplomat, that you are running the most ghastly risks on earth."

"In what direction?"

The young American shrugged his shoulders.

"Well, you've got a thoroughly democratic Government—not such a bad Government, I should say, as things go. They've bled your *bourgeoisie* a bit, and serve 'em right, but with an empire to keep up you're losing all touch upon international politics. Your ambassadors have been exchanged for trade consuls, the whole of your secret service staff has been disbanded, you place your entire faith on this sacred League of Nations. Say, Dorminster, you're taking risks!"

"You mustn't forget," Dorminster replied, "that it was your country who started the League of Nations."

"President Wilson did," Chalmers grunted. "You can't say that the country ever backed him up. That's the worst of us on the other side— we so seldom really get a common voice."

"The League of Nations was a thundering good idea," Nigel declared, "but it belongs to Utopia and not to this vulgar planet."

"Just so," Chalmers rejoined, "and yet you are about the only nation who ever took it into her bosom and suckled it. To be perfectly frank with you, now, what other nation in the world is there, except yours, which is obeying the conventions strictly? I tell you frankly, we keep our eye on Japan, and we build a good many commercial ships which would astonish you if you examined them thoroughly. Our National Guard, too, know a bit more about soldiering than their grandfathers. You people, on the other hand, seem to have become infatuated pacifists. I can't tell tales out of school, but I don't like the way things are going on eastwards. Asia means something different now that that amazing fellow, Prince Shan, has made a great nation of China."

"I am entirely in accord with you," Nigel agreed, "but what is one to do about it? Our present Government has a big majority, trade at home and abroad is prosperous, the income tax is down to a shilling in the pound and looks like being wiped out altogether. Everybody is fat and happy."

"Just as they were in 1914," Chalmers remarked significantly.

"More so," Dorminster asserted. "In those days we had our alarmists. Nowadays, they too seem to have gone to sleep. My uncle—"

"Your uncle was an uncommonly shrewd man," Chalmers interrupted. "I was going to talk about him."

"After lunch," Nigel suggested, rising to his feet. "Here come my cousin and some of her tennis friends. Karschoff is lunching with us, too. You know him, don't you? Come along and I'll introduce you to the others."

It was a very cheerful party who, after a few minutes under the trees, strolled into luncheon and took their places at the round table reserved for them at the end of the room. Maggie at once took possession of Chalmers.

"I have been so anxious to meet you, Mr. Chalmers," she said. "They tell me that you represent the modern methods in American diplomacy, and that therefore you have been made first secretary over the heads of half a dozen of your seniors. How they must dislike you, and how clever you must be!"

"I don't know that I'm so much disliked," the young man answered, with a twinkle in his eyes, "but I flatter myself that I have brought a new note into diplomacy. I was always taught that there were thirty-seven different ways of telling a lie, which is to state a diplomatic fact. I have swept them all away. I tell the truth."

"How daring," Maggie murmured, "and how wonderfully original! What should you say, now, if I asked you if my nose wanted powdering?"

"I should start by saying that the question was outside the sphere of my activities," he decided. "I should then proceed to add, as a private person, that a little dab on the left side would do it no harm."

"I begin to believe," she confessed, "that all I have heard of you is true."

"Tell me exactly what you have heard," he begged. "Leave out everything that isn't nice. I thrive on praise and good reports."

"To begin with, then, that you are an extraordinarily shrewd young man," she replied, "that you speak seven languages perfectly and know your way about every capital of Europe, and that you have ideas of your own as to what is going to happen during the next six or seven years."

"You've been moving in well-informed circles," he admitted. "Now shall I proceed to turn the tables upon you?"

"You can't possibly know anything about me," she declared confidently.

"I could tell you what I've discovered from personal observation," he replied.

"That sounds like compliments or candour," she murmured. "I'm terrified of both."

"Well, I guess I'm not out to frighten you," he assured her. "I'll keep the secrets of my heart hidden—until after luncheon, at any rate—and just ask you—how you enjoyed your stay in Berlin?"

Maggie's manner changed. She lowered her voice.

"In Berlin?" she repeated.

"In the household of the erstwhile leather manufacturer, the present President, Herr Essendorf. I hope you liked those fat children. They always seemed to me loathsome little brats."

"What do you know about my stay in Berlin?" she demanded.

"Everything there is to be known," he answered. "To tell you the truth, our people there were a trifle anxious about you. I was the little angel watching from above."

"You are, without a doubt," Maggie pronounced, "a most interesting young man. We will talk together presently."

"A hint which sends me back to my mutton," the young man observed. "Dorminster," he added, turning to his host, "I heard the other day, on very good authority, that you were thinking of writing a novel. If you are, study the lady who has just entered. There is a type for you, an intelligence which might baffle even your attempts at analysis."

Naida, escorted by her father and Immelan, took her place at an adjacent table. She bowed to Nigel and Karschoff before sitting down, and her eyes travelled over the rest of the party with interest. Then she recognised Maggie and waved her hand.

"Immelan is a very constant admirer," Prince Karschoff remarked, a little uneasily.

"Is that her father?" Maggie asked.

The Prince nodded.

"He is one of the ambassadors of commerce from my country," he said. "In place of diplomacy, he superintends the exchange of shipping cargoes and talks freights. I suppose Immelan and he are all the time comparing notes, but I scarcely see where my dear friend Naida comes in."

"There is still the oldest interest in the world for her to fall back upon," Chalmers murmured. "One hears that Immelan is devoted."

"Scandalmonger!" the Prince declared severely. "Young man from the New World," he proceeded, "get on with your lunch and drink your iced water. Let the vision of those two remind you that it was your people who foisted the League of Nations upon us, and be humble, even sorrowful, when you view one of the sad results."

"I can't be responsible, directly or indirectly, for a political flirtation," Chalmers grumbled. "Besides, why should there be any politics about it at all? Mademoiselle Karetsky is quite attractive enough to turn the head even of a seasoned old boulevardier like you, Prince."

"That young man," Karschoff said deliberately, "will find himself before long face to face with a blighted career. He has no respect for age, and he is shockingly lacking in finesse. All the same, on one point I am agreed. I don't think there is a man breathing who could resist Naida if she wished to call him to her."

The little party broke up presently and wandered out into the gardens. They sat for a while upon the lawn, drinking their coffee and exchanging greetings with acquaintances. In the distance, the orchestra was playing soft music, with a fine regard for the atmosphere of the pleasant, almost languorous spring afternoon. Everywhere were signs of contentment, even gaiety, and here the alien streak of unfamiliar newcomers was far less pronounced. When the time came for tennis, Chalmers led the way with Maggie. As soon as they were out of hearing of the others, she turned towards him a little abruptly.

"Tell me exactly what you know about my stay in Berlin," she demanded.

"Everything," he answered gravely.

"You mean?"

"I mean that the New World to-day has progressed where the Old World seems to have been stricken with a terrible blindness. Our secret-service system has never been better, and frankly I hear many things which I don't like. I am going to talk to Lord Dorminster this afternoon very seriously, but in the meantime I wanted to speak to you. I heard a rumour that you thought of going back to Berlin."

"I don't know how you heard it, but the rumour is not altogether untrue," she admitted. "I have not yet made up my mind."

"Don't go," he begged.

"You think they really do know all about me?"

"I know that they do. I don't mind telling you that you had the shave of your life on the Dutch frontier last time, and I don't mind telling you, also, that we had two of our men shadowing you. One of them acted on his own initiative, or you would never have crossed the frontier."

"I rather wondered why they let me out," she observed. "Perhaps you can explain why Frau Essendorf keeps on writing to me under my pseudonym of 'Miss Brown' and to my reputed address in Lincolnshire, begging me to return."

"I could tell you that, too," he replied. "They want you back in Berlin."

"They really do know, then, that I brought over the dispatch from Atcheson?" she asked.

"They know it," he assured her. "They know, too, that it was chiefly a wasted labour. Their London agents saw to that."

"Perhaps," she suggested, "you know who their London agents are?"

"Sooner or later in our conversation," he remarked, "we were bound to arrive at a point—"

"Come along and let us make up a set then," she intervened.

VII

Naida, deserted by her father, who had found a taxicab to take him back to the purlieus of Piccadilly and auction bridge, sauntered along at the back of the tennis nets until she arrived at the court where Nigel and his party were playing.

"I should like to watch this game for a few minutes," she told her companion. "The men are such opposite types and yet both so good-looking. And Lady Maggie fascinates me."

Immelan fetched two chairs, and they settled down to watch the set. Nigel, with his clean, well-knit figure, looked his best in spotless white flannels. Chalmers, a more powerful and muscular type, also presented a fine appearance. The play was fast and sometimes brilliant. Nigel had Maggie for a partner, and Chalmers one of her friends, and the set was as nearly equal as possible. Naida leaned forward in her chair, following every stroke with interest.

"I find this most fascinating," she murmured. "I hope that Lord Dorminster and his cousin will win. Your sympathies, of course, are on the other side."

"You are right," Immelan assented. "My sympathies are on the other side."

There was a lull in the game for a moment or two. The sun was troublesome, and the players were changing courts. Naida turned towards her companion thoughtfully.

"My friend," she said, glancing around as though to be sure that they were not overheard, "there are times when you move me to wonder. In the small things as well as the large, you are so unchanging. I think that you would see an Englishman die, whether he were your friend or your enemy, very much as you kick a poisonous snake out of your path."

"It is quite true," was the calm reply.

"But America was once your enemy," she continued, watching Chalmers' powerful service.

"With America we made peace," he explained. "With England, never. If you would really appreciate and understand the reason for that undying hatred which I and millions of my fellow countrymen feel, it will cost you exactly one shilling. Go to any stationer's and buy a copy of the Treaty of Versailles. Read it word by word and line by line. It is the most brutal document that was ever printed. It will help you to understand."

She nodded slowly.

"Paul always declared," she said, "that in those days England had no statesmen—no one who could feel what lay beyond the day-by-day horizon. When I think of that Treaty, my friend, I sympathise with you. It is not a great thing to forge chains of hate for a beaten enemy."

"If you realise this, are you not then our friend?" Immelan asked.

She appeared for a few moments to be engrossed in the tennis. Her companion, however, waited for her answer.

"In a way," she acknowledged, "I find something magnificent in your wonderfully conceived plans for vengeance, and in the spirit which has evolved and kept them alive through all these years. Then, on the other hand, I look at home, and I ask myself whether you do not make what they would call over here a cat's-paw of my country."

"Ours is the most natural and most beneficial of all possible alliances," Immelan insisted. "Germany and Russia, hand in hand, can dominate the world."

"I am not sure that it is an equal bargain, though, which you seek to drive with us," she said. "Germany aims, of course, at world power, but you are still fettered by the terms of that Treaty. You cannot build a great fleet of warships or æroplanes; you cannot train great armies; you cannot lay up for yourselves all the store that is necessary for a successful war. So you bring your brains to Russia, and you ask us to do these things; but Russia does not aim at world power. Russia seeks only for a great era of self-development. She, too, has a mighty neighbour at her gates. I am not sure that your bargain is a fair one."

"It is the first time that I have heard you talk like this," Immelan declared, with a little tremor in his tone.

"I have been in England twice during the last few months," Naida said. "You know very well at whose wish I came, I have been studying the conditions here, studying the people so far as I can. I find them such a kindly race. I find their present Government so unsuspicious, so genuinely altruistic. After all, that Treaty belongs to an England that has passed. The England of to-day would never go to war at all. They believe here that they have solved the problem of perpetual peace."

Immelan smiled a little bitterly.

"Dear lady," he said, "if I lose your help, if you go back to Petrograd and talk to Paul Matinsky as you are talking to me, do you know that you will break the heart of a nation?"

She shook her head.

"Paul does not look upon me as infallible," she protested. "Besides, there are other considerations. And now, please, we will talk of the tennis. I do not know whether it is my fancy, but that man there to your left, in grey, seems to me to be taking an interest in our conversation. He cannot possibly overhear, and he has not glanced once in our direction, yet I have an instinct for these things."

Immelan glanced in the direction of the stranger,—a quiet-looking, spare man dressed in a grey tweed suit, clean-shaven and of early middle-age. There was nothing about his appearance to distinguish him from a score or more of other loiterers.

"You are quite right," her companion admitted. "One should not talk of these things even where the birds may listen, but it is so difficult. As for that man, he could not possibly hear, but there might be others. One passes behind on the grass so noiselessly."

They relapsed into silence. Naida, leaning a little forward, became once more engrossed in the play. Her eyes were fixed upon Nigel. It was his movements which she followed, his strokes which she usually applauded. Immelan sat by her side and watched.

"They are well matched," he remarked presently.

"Mr. Chalmers has a wonderful service," she declared, "but Lord Dorminster has more skill. Oh, bravo!"

The set at that moment was finished by a backhanded return from Nigel, which skimmed over the net at a great pace, completely out of reach of the opposing couple. The players strolled across to the seats under the trees. Naida smiled at Nigel, and he came over to her side. Once again he was conscious of that peculiar sense of pleasure and well-being which he felt in her company.

"You play tennis very well, Lord Dorminster," she said.

"I found inspiration," he answered.

"In your partner?"

"Maggie is always charming to play with. I was thinking of the onlookers."

"Mr. Immelan is very interested in tennis," she remarked, with a smile which challenged him.

"And you?"

"Even more so."

"Tell me about games in Russia," he begged, seating himself on the grass by her side.

"We have none," she replied. "I learnt my tennis at Cannes, where, curiously enough, I saw you play three years ago."

"You were there then?" he asked with interest.

"For a few days only. We were motoring from Spain to Monte Carlo. Cannes was very crowded, but you see I remembered."

Her voice seemed to have some lingering charm in it, some curiously potent suggestion of personal interest which stirred his pulses. He looked up and met her eyes. For a moment the world of tennis fields, of pleasant chatter and of holiday-makings, passed away. He rose abruptly to his feet. This time he avoided looking at her.

"You must come over and speak to Maggie," he begged. "Perhaps Mr. Immelan will spare you for a few moments."

Immelan bowed, sphinxlike but coldly furious. The two strolled away together.

When the next set was over, Naida, who had rejoined her companion, had disappeared. On one of their vacated chairs was seated the quiet-looking stranger in grey. Chalmers passed his arm through Nigel's and led him in that direction.

"I want you two to know each other," he said. "Jesson, this is Lord Dorminster—Mr. Gilbert Jesson—Lord Dorminster."

The two men shook hands, Nigel a little vaguely. He was at first unable to place this newcomer.

"Mr. Jesson," Chalmers explained, dropping his voice a little, "was a highly privileged and very much valued member of our Intelligence Department, until he resigned a few months ago. I think that if you could spare an hour or two any time this evening, Dorminster, it would interest you very much to know exactly the reason for Mr. Jesson's resignation."

"I should be very pleased indeed," Nigel replied. "Won't you both come and dine in Belgrave Square to-night? I was going to ask you, anyhow, Chalmers. Naida Karetsky has promised to come, and my cousin will be hostess."

"It will give me very great pleasure," Jesson acquiesced. "You will understand," he added, "that the information which Mr. Chalmers has just given you concerning myself is entirely confidential."

Nigel nodded.

"We three will have a little talk to ourselves afterwards," he suggested. "At eight o'clock—Number 17, Belgrave Square."

Jesson strolled away after a little desultory conversation. Chalmers looked after him thoughtfully.

"Harmless-looking chap, isn't he?" he observed. "Yet I'll let you in on this, Dorminster: there isn't another living person who knows so much of what is going on behind the scenes in Europe as that man."

"Why has he chucked his job, then?" Nigel enquired.

"He will tell you that to-night," was Chalmers' quiet reply.

VIII

"I don't think I shall marry you, after all," Maggie announced that evening, as she stood looking at herself in one of the gilded mirrors with which the drawing-room at Belgrave Square was adorned.

"Why not?" Nigel asked, with polite anxiety.

"You are exhibiting symptoms of infidelity," she declared. "Your flirtation with Naida this afternoon was most pronounced, and you went out of your way to ask her to dine to-night."

"I like that!" Nigel complained. "Supposing it were true, I should simply be obeying orders. It was you who incited me to devote myself to her."

"The sacrifices we women make for the good of our country," Maggie sighed. "However, you needn't have taken me quite so literally. Do you admire her very much, Nigel?"

He smiled. His manner, however, was not altogether free from self-consciousness.

"Of course I do," he admitted. "She's a perfectly wonderful person, isn't she? Let's get out of this Victorian environment," he added, looking around the huge apartment with its formal arrangement of furniture and its atmosphere of prim but faded elegance. "We'll go into the smaller room and tell Brookes to bring us some cocktails and cigarettes. Chalmers won't expect to be received formally, and Mademoiselle Karetsky will appreciate the cosmopolitan note of our welcome."

"We do look a little too domestic, don't we?" Maggie replied, as she passed through the portière which Nigel was holding up. "I'm not at all sure that I ought to come and play hostess like this, without an aunt or anything. I must think of my reputation. I may decide to marry Mr. Chalmers, and Americans are very particular about that sort of thing."

"From what I have seen of him, I should think that Chalmers would make you an excellent husband," Nigel declared, as he rang the bell. "You need a firm hand, and I should think he would be quite capable of using it."

"You take the matter far too calmly," she objected. "I can assure you that I am getting peevish. I hate all Russian women with creamy complexions and violet-coloured eyes."

"They are wonderful eyes," Nigel declared, after he had given Brookes an order.

Maggie looked at him curiously.

"Naida is for your betters, sir," she reminded him. "You must not forget that she is to rule over Russia some day."

"Just at present," Nigel observed, "Paul Matinsky has a perfectly good wife of his own."

"An invalid."

"Invalids always live long."

"Presidents and emperors can always get divorces," Maggie insisted, "especially in this irreligious age."

"Matinsky isn't that sort," Nigel said cheerfully. "Even an old gossip like Karschoff calls him a purist, and you yourself have spoken of his principles."

Maggie shrugged her shoulders.

"All right," she remarked. "If you are determined to rush into danger, I suppose you must. There is just one more point to be considered, though. I suppose you know that if you succeed any farther with Naida, you will introduce a personal note into our coming struggle."

"What do you mean?" Nigel demanded.

"Why, Immelan, of course," she replied. "He's head over ears in love with Naida. Any one can see that."

Nigel laughed scornfully.

"My dear child," he protested, "can you imagine a woman like Naida thinking seriously of a fellow like Immelan?—a scheming, Teutonic adventurer, without even the breeding of his class!"

Maggie laughed softly for several moments.

"My dear Nigel," she exclaimed, "what a luxury to get at the man of you! I haven't seen your eyes flash like that for ages. The cocktails, thank goodness! Shake one for me till it froths all the way up the glass, please, and then give me a cigarette."

Nigel obeyed orders, helped himself, and glanced at the clock as Brookes left the room.

"How nice of you to come half an hour early, Maggie!" he remarked.

She made a little grimace.

"The first time you have noticed it," she said dolefully. "Do you realise, Nigel, that it is nearly a week since you proposed to me? Apart from your penchant for Naida, don't you really want to marry me any more?"

He came across the room and stood looking down at her thoughtfully. She was wearing a somewhat daringly fashioned black lace gown, which showed a good deal of her white shoulders and neck. Her brown hair was simply but artistically arranged. She was piquante, alluring, with a provocative smile at the corners of her lips and a challenging gleam in her eyes. The daintiness and femininity of her were enthralling.

"You would make an adorable wife," he reflected.

"For some one else?"

"An unspeakable proposition," he assured her.

"You're very nice-looking, Nigel," she murmured.

"You're terribly attractive, Maggie!"

"Then why is it," she sighed, "that we neither of us want to marry the other?"

"If a serious proposition would really be of interest to you," he began,—

She made a little grimace.

"You heard them coming," she interrupted.

The three expected guests arrived almost together, bringing with them, at any rate so far as Chalmers and Naida were concerned, an atmosphere of light-heartedness which was later on to make the little dinner party a complete success. Naida, too, was in black, a gown simpler than Maggie's but full of distinction. She wore no jewellery except a wonderful string of pearls. Her black hair was brushed straight back from her forehead but drooped a little over her ears. She seemed to bring with her a larger share of girlishness than any of them had previously observed in her, as though she had made up her mind for this one evening to cast herself adrift from the graver cares of life and to indulge in the frivolities which after all were the heritage of her youth. She sat at Nigel's right hand and plied him with questions as to the lighter side of his life,—his favourite sport, books, and general occupation. She gave evidences of humour which delighted everybody, and Nigel, though he would at times have welcomed, and did his best to initiate, an incursion into more serious subjects, found himself compelled to admire the tact with which she continually foiled him.

"It is a mistake," she declared once, "to believe that a woman is ever serious unless she is forced to be. All our natural proclivities are towards gaiety. We are really butterflies by instinct, and we are at our best when we are natural. Don't you agree with me, Maggie?"

"From the bottom of my heart," Maggie assented. "Nothing but conscience ever induces me to pull a long face and turn my thoughts to serious things. And I haven't a great deal of conscience."

"So you see," Naida continued, smiling up at her host, "when you try to get a woman to talk politics or sociology with you, you are brushing a little of the down off her wings. We really want to be told—other things."

"I should imagine," he replied, "that my sex frequently indulged you."

"Not so much as I should desire," she assured him. "I have somehow or other acquired an undeserved reputation for brains. In Russia especially, when I meet a stranger, they don't even look at my frock or the way my hair is done. They plunge instead into a subject of which I know nothing—philosophy or history, or international politics."

"Do you know nothing of international politics?" Nigel asked.

"A home thrust," she declared, laughing. "I suppose that is a subject upon which I have some glimmerings of knowledge. Really not very much, though, but then I have a theory about that. I think sometimes that the clearest judgments are formed by some one who comes a little fresh to a subject, some one who hasn't been dabbling in it half their lifetime and acquired prejudices. Do you always provide strawberries for your guests, Lord Dorminster? If so, I should like to come and live here."

"If you will promise to come and live here," he replied, "I will provide strawberries if I have to start a nursery garden in Jersey."

"Maggie," Naida announced across the table, "Lord Dorminster has proposed to me. The matter of strawberries has brought us together. I don't think I shall accept him. There are no means of making him keep his bargain."

"He'd make an awfully good husband," Maggie declared. "If no one else wants me, I shall probably marry him myself some day."

Naida shook her head.

"Lord Dorminster is more my type," she declared. "Besides, you have had your chance if you really wanted him. I have a great friend in Russia who prophesies that I shall never marry. That does not please me. I think not to be married is the worst fate that can happen to any woman."

"The remedy," Nigel told her, "is in your own hands."

Jesson, quieter than the others, was still an interesting personality, often intervening with a shrewd remark and listening to the sallies of the others with a humorous gleam in his spectacle-shielded eyes. When at last the girls left them for a time, Nigel led the way at once into the library, where coffee and liqueurs were served.

"I expect the others will find their way here in a few minutes," he said, as the door closed behind Brookes and his satellite. "You had something to say to me, Chalmers, about Mr. Jesson here."

"All that I have to say is in the nature of a testimonial," the young American replied. "Jesson was easily one of our best men in Europe. He resigned a few months ago simply because he wants a job with you fellows."

"I don't quite understand," Nigel began.

"Let me explain," Jesson begged. "I spent the last three years poking about Europe, and so far as the United States is concerned, there's nothing doing. My reports aren't worth much more than the paper they are written on, and while I'm drawing my money from Washington, it's not my business to collect information that affects other countries. That's why I've sent in my resignation. There are great events brewing eastwards, Lord Dorminster, and I want to take a hand in the game."

"Do you want to work for us?" Nigel asked.

"You're right," was the quiet reply. "I guess that's how I've figured it out. You see, I'm one of those Americans who still consider themselves half English. Next to the United States, Great Britain is the country for me. I know what I'm talking about, Lord Dorminster, and I've come to the conclusion that there's a lot of trouble in store for you people."

"I'm pretty well convinced of that myself," Nigel agreed, "but you know how things are with us. We have a democratic Government who have placed their whole faith in the League of Nations, and who are absolutely and entirely anti-militarist. On paper, the governments of Russia, Germany, and most of the other countries of Europe, are of the same ilk. Some of us—my uncle was one—who have studied history and who know something of the science of international politics, realise perfectly well that no Empire can be considered secure under such conditions. This country swarms with foreign secret-service men. What they are planning against us, Heaven knows!"

"Heaven and Naida Karetsky," Chalmers intervened softly.

"You believe that she is our enemy?" Nigel asked, with a look of trouble in his eyes.

"She is Immelan's friend," Chalmers reminded him.

"There was a man named Atcheson," Jesson began quietly—
Nigel nodded.

"He was one of the men my uncle sent out. The first one was stabbed in Petrograd. Jim Atcheson was poisoned and died in Berlin."

"There was rather a scare in a certain quarter about Atcheson," Jesson observed. "He was supposed to have got a report through to the late Lord Dorminster."

"He got it through all right," Nigel replied. "My uncle was busy decoding it, seated in this room, at that table, when he died."

"His death was very sudden," Jesson ventured.

"I have not the faintest doubt but that he was murdered," Nigel declared. "The document upon which he was working disappeared entirely except for one sheet."

"You have that one sheet?" Jesson asked eagerly.

Nigel produced it from his pocketbook, smoothed it cut, and laid it upon the table.

"There are two things worth noticing here," he pointed out. "The first is that the actual name of a town in Russia is given, and a telephone number in London. Kroten I have looked up on the map. It seems to be an unimportant place in a very desolate region. The telephone number is Oscar Immelan's."

"That is interesting, though not surprising," Jesson declared. "Immelan, as you of course know, is one of your enemies, one of those who are working in this country for purposes of his own. But as regards Kroten, may I ask where you obtained your information about the place?"

Nigel dragged down the atlas and showed them the paragraph. Jesson read it with a faint smile upon his lips.

"I fancy," he remarked, "that this is a little out of date. I should like, if you have no objection, to start for Kroten this week."

"Good heavens! Why?" Nigel exclaimed.

"I can scarcely answer that question," Jesson said. "I am like a man with a puzzle board and a heap of loose pieces. Kroten is one of those pieces, but I haven't commenced the fitting-in process yet. Here," he said, "is as much as I can tell you about it. There are three cities, situated in different countries in the world, which are each in their way connected with the danger which is brewing for this country. I have heard them described as the three secret cities. One is in Germany. I have been there at the risk of my life, and I came away simply puzzled. Kroten is the next, and of the third I have still to discover the whereabouts. Are you willing, Lord Dorminster, to let me act for you abroad? I require no salary or remuneration of any sort. I am a wealthy man, and investigations of this kind are my one hobby. I shall not move without your permission, although I recognise, of course, that your own position is entirely an unofficial one. If you will trust me, however, I promise that all my energies shall be devoted to the interests of this country."

Nigel held out his hand.

"It is a pact," he decided. "Before you leave, I will give you the whole of my uncle's brief correspondence with Sidwell. You may be able to gather from it what he was after. Sidwell, you remember, was stabbed in a café in the slums of Petrograd."

"I remember quite well," Jesson admitted quietly. "I knew Sidwell. He was a clever person in his way, but he relied too much upon disguises. I fancy that I hear the voices of the ladies coming. I shall just have time to tell you rather a curious coincidence."

The two men waited eagerly. Jesson touched with his forefinger the sheet of paper which he had been studying.

"Sidwell," he concluded, "could not have been so far off the mark. The man with whom he was spending the evening in that café was a mechanic from Kroten."

IX

Naida, early one afternoon, a few days after the dinner at Belgrave Square, raised herself on one elbow from the sofa on which she was resting, glanced at the roses and the card which the maid had presented for her inspection, and waved them impatiently away.

"The gentleman waits," the woman reminded her.

Naida glanced out of the window across a dull and apparently uninviting prospect of roofs and chimneys, to where in the background a faint line of silver and a wheeling flock of sea gulls became dimly visible through the branches of the distant trees. The window itself was flung wide open, but the slowly moving air had little of freshness in it. Sparrows twittered around the window-sill, and a little patch of green shone out from the Embankment Gardens. The radiance of spring here found few opportunities.

"The gentleman waits," the serving woman repeated stolidly, speaking in her native Russian.

"You can show him up," her mistress replied a little wearily.

Immelan entered, a few moments later, spruce and neat in a well-fitting grey suit, and carrying a grey Homburg hat. He was redolent of soaps and perfumes. His step was buoyant, almost jaunty, yet in his blue eyes, as he bent over the hand of the woman upon whom he had come to call, lurked something of the disquietude which, notwithstanding his most strenuous efforts, was beginning to assert itself.

"You make me very happy, my dear Naida," he began, "that you receive me thus so informally. Your good father is smoking in the lounge. He bade me come up."

She beckoned him to a seat.

"A thousand thanks for your flowers, my friend," she said. "Now tell me why you are possessed to see me at this untimely hour. I always rest for a time after luncheon, and I am only here because the sunshine filled my room and made me restless."

"There is a little matter of news," he announced slowly. "I thought it might interest you. I hoped it would."

She turned her head and looked at him.

"News?" she repeated. "News from you means only one thing. Is it good or bad?"

"It is good," he replied, "because it saves me a long and tedious journey, because it saves me also from a separation which I should have found detestable."

"Your journey to China, then, is abandoned?"

"It is rendered unnecessary. Prince Shan has decided after all to adhere to his original plan and come to Europe."

"You are sure?"

"I have an official intimation," he replied. "I may probably have to go to Paris, but no farther. It is even possible that I might leave to-night."

She was genuinely interested.

"There is no one in the whole world," she declared, "whom I have wanted to meet so much as Prince Shan."

"You will not be disappointed," he promised her. "There is no one like him. When he enters the room, you know that you are in the presence of a great man. The three of us together! Naida, we will remake the map of the world."

She frowned a little uneasily.

"Do not take too much for granted, Oscar," she enjoined. "Remember that I am here to watch and to report. It is not for me to make decisions."

"Then for whom else?" he demanded. "Paul Matinsky himself wrote me that you had his entire confidence—that you possessed full powers for action. You will not be faint-hearted, Naida?"

"I shall never be false to my convictions," she replied.

There was a brief silence. He was not altogether satisfied, but he judged the moment unpropitious for any further reference to the coming of Prince Shan.

"My plans, as you see, are changed," he said at last, "and for that reason a promise which I made to myself will not now be kept."

She rose to her feet a little uneasily, shook out her fluffy morning gown, and retreated towards the door leading to the apartments beyond. He watched her without movement. She picked up a pile of letters from a table in the middle of the room, glanced at them, and threw them down.

"It is as well," she warned him, "to keep all promises."

"As for this one," he replied, "I have no responsibility save to myself. I absolve myself. I give myself permission to speak. Your father is even wishful that I should do so. I crave from you, Naida, the happiness which only you can bring into my life. I ask you to become my wife."

She looked at him without visible change of expression. Her lips, however, were a little parted. The air of aloofness with which she moved through the world seemed suddenly more marked. He would have been a brave man, or one entirely without perceptions, who would have advanced towards her at that moment.

"That is quite impossible," she pronounced.

"I do not admit it," he contended. "No, I will never admit that. The fates brought us together. It will take something stronger than fate to drive us apart. I had not meant to speak yet. I had meant to wait until the great pact was sealed and the glory to come assured, but during these last few days I have suffered. A strange fancy has come to me. I seem to feel something between us, so I speak before it can grow. I speak because without you life for me would be a thing not worth having. You are my life and my soul. You will not send me away?"

Naida was troubled but unhesitating. It was perhaps at that moment that a hidden characteristic of her features showed itself. Her mouth, sometimes almost too voluptuous in its softness, had straightened into a firm line of scarlet. The deeper violet of her eyes had gone. So a woman might have looked who watched suffering unmoved, the woman of the bull or prize fight.

"I am glad that you have spoken, Oscar," she said. "I know a thing now which has been a source of doubt and anxiety to me. What you ask is impossible. I do not love you. I shall never love you. A few days ago, I asked myself the very question you have just asked me, and I could not answer it. Now I know."

Pain and anger struggled in his face. He was suffering, without a doubt, but for a moment it seemed as though the anger would predominate. His great shoulders heaved, his hands were clenched until the signet ring on his left finger cut into the flesh, his eyes were like glittering points of fire.

"It is the old dream concerning Paul?" he demanded.

"It has nothing to do with Paul," she assured him. "Concerning him I will admit that I have had my weak moments. I think that those have passed. It was such a wonderful dream," she went on reflectively, "the dream of ruling the mightiest nation in the world, a nation that even now, after many years of travail, is only just finding its way through to the light. It seemed such a small thing that stood in the way. Since then I have met Paul's wife. She does not understand, but at least she loves."

"She is a poor fool, no helpmate for any man," Immelan declared. "Yet it is not his cause I plead, but mine. I, too, can minister to your ambitions. Be my wife, and I swear to you that before five years have passed I will be President of the German Republic. Germany is no strange country to you," he went on passionately. "It is you who have helped in the great *rapprochement*. At times when Paul has been difficult, you have smoothed the way. I would not speak against your country, I would not speak against anything which lies close to your heart, but let me tell you that when the day of purification comes, the day when God gives us leave to pour out the vials of vengeance, there will be no prouder, no more glorious people than ours. Our triumph will be yours, Naida. You yourself will help to cement the great alliance of these years."

She shook her head.

"I am a woman," she said simply. "Incidentally, I am a politician and something of an altruist, but when it comes to marriage, I am a woman. I do not love you, Oscar, and I will not marry you."

There was a darker shade upon his face now. Unconsciously he had drawn a little nearer to her.

"Listen," he begged; "it is perhaps possible that I have not been mistaken—that a certain change has crept up in you even within the last few days? Tell me, is there any one else who has found his way into your heart? No, I will not say heart! It could not be your heart in so short a time. Into your fancy? Is there any one else, Naida, of whom you are thinking?"

"That is my concern, Oscar, and mine only," she answered haughtily.

A weaker woman he would have bullied. His veins were filled with anger. His tongue ached to spend itself. Naida's bearing cowed him. She remained a dominating figure. The unnatural restraint imposed upon himself, however, made his voice sound hard and unfamiliar. There were little patches of white around his mouth; his teeth showed, when he spoke, more than usual.

"If there were any one else," he declared, "and that some one else should chance to be an Englishman, I would find a new hell for him."

"There is no one else," she answered calmly, "but if there ever should be, Oscar Immelan, and if you ever interfered with him, either in this country or any other, my arm would follow you around the world. Remember that."

She turned away for a moment, eager to gain a brief respite from his darkening face. When she looked around, he was gone. She heard his footsteps passing down the corridor, the bell ringing for the lift, the clank of the gates as he stepped in. Once more she gazed out over the uninspiring prospect. There was a little more sunshine upon the river; more of the dusty chimney-pots seemed bathed in its silvery radiance. As she stood there, she felt herself growing calmer. The tension passed from her nerves. Her eyes grew soft again. Then an impulse came to her. She stretched out her hand for the telephone book, turned over the pages restlessly, looked through the "D's" until she found the name for which she was searching. For a long time she hesitated. When at last she took up the receiver and asked for a number, she was conscious of a slight thrill, a sense of excitement which in moments of more complete self-control would at least have served as a warning to her.

X

The curtain fell upon the first act of "Louise." The lights were turned up, the tenseness relaxed, men made dives for their hats, and the unmusical murmured the usual platitudes. Naida leaned forward from the corner of her box to the man who was her sole companion.

"Father," she said, "I am expecting a caller with whom I wish to speak—Lord Dorminster. If he comes, will you leave us alone? And if any one else should be here, please take them away."

"More mysteries," her father muttered, not unkindly. "Who is this man Dorminster?"

Naida leaned back in her chair and fanned herself slowly.

"No one I know very much about," she acknowledged. "I have selected him in my mind, however as being a typical Englishman of his class. I wish to talk to him, to appreciate his point of view. You know what Paul said when he gave you the appointment and sent us over here: 'Find out for me what sort of men these Englishmen are.'"

"Matinsky should know," her father observed. "He was here twelve years ago. He came over with the first commission which established regular relations with the British Government."

"No doubt," she said equably, "he was able to gauge the official outlook, but this country, during the last ten years, has gone through great vicissitudes. Besides, it is not only the official outlook in which Paul is interested. He doesn't understand, and frankly I don't, the position of what they call over here 'the man in the street.' You see, he must be either a fool, or he must be grossly deceived."

"So far as my dealings with him go, I should never call the Englishman a fool," Karetsky confessed.

"There are degrees and conditions of fools," his daughter declared calmly. "A man with a perfectly acute brain may have simply idiotic impulses towards credulity, and a credulous man is always a fool. Anyhow, I know what Paul wants."

There was a knock at the door. Karetsky opened it and stood aside to let Nigel pass in. Naida held out her hand to the latter with a smile.

"I am so glad that you have come," she said, raising her eyes for a minute to his. "Father, you remember Lord Dorminster?"

The two men exchanged a few commonplace remarks. Then Karetsky reached for his hat.

"Your arrival, Lord Dorminster," he observed, "leaves me free to make a few calls myself. We shall, I trust, meet again."

Nigel murmured a few courteous words and watched the retreating figure with some curiosity.

"Your father is very typical," he declared. "He reminds me of your country itself. He is massive, has suggestions of undeveloped strength."

"Add that he is a little ponderous," Naida said lightly, "slow to make up his mind, but as obstinate as the Urals themselves, and you have described him. Now tell me what you think of a young woman who rings you up without the slightest encouragement and invites you to come to the Opera purposely to visit her box."

"I deny the absence of encouragement, and I am very grateful for the opportunity of coming," Nigel answered. "And if I were to tell you all that I think of you," he added, after a moment's pause, "it would take me a great deal longer than this quarter of an hour's interval."

These were their first few moments absolutely alone. Neither of them was unduly emotional, neither wholly free from experience, yet they looked and spoke and felt as though the coming of new things was at hand. The atmosphere of music, still present, was a wonderful background to the intensified sensations of which both were conscious. Naida had the utmost difficulty in steadying her voice.

"I wanted to talk to you seriously because you can help me very much if you will," she began. "In a sense, I am over here upon a mission. Some of us in Russia feel that your nation is imperfectly understood there. We are bearing grudges against you which may not be wholly justified. You see, to speak very plainly, we are under the constant influence of a people which cherishes no feelings of friendship towards you."

For a moment the personal element had disappeared. Nigel remembered who his companion was and all that she stood for. He drew his chair a little nearer to hers.

"If you are looking for a typical Englishman," he said, "I fear that I shall be a disappointment to you. The typical Englishman of to-day is hiding his head in the sand. I am not disposed to do anything of the sort. I recognise a great coming danger, and I am afraid of your country."

"The attitude of the official Englishman I know," she declared, a little eagerly. "What I want to find out is whether there are many like yourself, who are awake."

"I am afraid that I am in the minority," he confessed. "I am trying to carry on the work which my uncle commenced. I am trying to secure firm and definite evidence of a certain plot which I believe to be brewing in your country and in Germany."

"Tell me exactly what you know," she begged.

Nigel looked at her for several moments in silence. She was wearing a Russian headdress, a low tiara of bound coils of pearls. A rope of pearls hung from her neck. Her white net gown was trimmed with ermine. At her first appearance in the front of the box she had created almost a sensation among those to whom she was visible. In these darker shadows the sensuous disturbance of which he had been conscious since his entrance swept over him once more with overmastering power.

"You are very beautiful," he said, a little abruptly.

"I am glad you think so," she murmured, with a very sweet answering light in her eyes, "but I am hoping that you have other things to tell me."

"You are the friend of Immelan," he reminded her.

"To some extent, yes," she assented, "but I admit of no prejudices. The greatest friend I have in the world is Paul Matinsky, and it is at his wish that I am here. He is anxious above all things not to make a mistake."

"Your country is very much under the dominance of Germany," he ventured.

"Very much, I admit, but not utterly so. You must remember that after the cataclysm of 1917, Russia has been born again in travail and agony. No hand was outstretched to help her, save that of Germany alone, for her own sake ultimately, perhaps, but nevertheless with invaluable results to Russia. We had vast resources which Germany exploited, magnificent human material which Germany has educated and disciplined. The two nations have grown together for their common interest. At the same time, Paul Matinsky and very many others have always felt that there is one of Germany's great ambitions in which Russia ought not necessarily to become involved. I think—I hope that you understand me."

"In plain words," Nigel said, "you refer to this projected plan of isolating England."

"In plain words, I do," she admitted. "Russia's intentions concerning that are trembling in the balance. Germany is pressing her hard. Nothing will be finally decided until I return to Petrograd. You see, I speak to you quite openly, for I myself have had some experience of your present statesmen. I believe if you were to repeat this conversation to any one of them, if, even, you could open their eyes to what is happening, they would only shrug their shoulders and say that they relied for their protection on the League of Nations."

"You are unhappily right," Nigel groaned, "yet one perseveres, and after all there is an element of mystery about the whole affair. The French, as you know, have not imitated our blind credulity. Their frontier would seem to be impregnable, and the difficulties of invading England, even from the air, are very much as they were during the last war. It was these considerations which made my uncle persevere in his attempt at secret-service work on the Continent. Everything depends upon our knowing exactly what is in store for us."

"And have you discovered that?" she enquired.

He shook his head.

"Everything that we have learnt so far has been of negative value," he replied. "The German citizen army is large, but not threateningly so. So far as we have been able to discover, they do not seem to have any secret store of guns or ammunition. Their docks hold no secrets. Yet we know that there is something brewing. Both the men upon whom my uncle relied have been murdered."

"But one of them succeeded in getting a dispatch through, did he not?" she asked quietly.

"Yes, he succeeded," Nigel acknowledged. "My uncle was murdered, however, in the act of decoding it, and the dispatch itself was stolen."

"You are very frank," she said. "I suppose I ought to feel flattered that you treat me with so little reserve."

"If you are a friend to Germany," he replied, "you probably know all that I can tell you. If you are inclined towards friendship with us, then it is as well that you should know everything."

"That is reasonable," she admitted. "Now listen. This conversation can only last a few minutes longer. It is true that Oscar Immelan is my father's old friend and also mine, but my judgment in all matters which relate to the welfare of my country is not influenced by that fact."

"There was a report once," Nigel said, taking his courage into both hands, "that you were engaged to be married to him."

She looked him in the eyes. Against the whiteness of his skin, the colour of her own seemed more wonderful than ever.

"That is not true," she replied. "It will never be true."

"I am glad," he declared fervently.

There was a brief pause. Both seemed conscious of a renewal of that air of disturbance which had reigned between them during their first

　　　　　　　　　　　　　　　　　E. PHILLIPS OPPENHEIM

few moments alone. It was Naida who made an effort to restore their conversation to its former tone.

"If Germany has any scheme against this country," she said, "believe me, it will not be so obvious as you seem to think. It will be a scheme which can only be carried out with the assistance of other countries, and that assistance is not yet wholly promised. I cannot betray to you my knowledge of certain things," she went on, after a moment's hesitation, "but I can at least give you this warning. It is not for his health alone that Prince Shan is flying from China to Paris. If there is a single member of your Government who has the least apprehension of world politics, now is the time for action."

"There is no one," Nigel answered gloomily.

The box was suddenly invaded. Karetsky reappeared with several other men. In the rear of the little procession came Immelan. His face darkened as he recognised Nigel. Naida looked across at him with a slight frown upon her forehead.

"You have changed your mind?" she remarked. "I thought you were for Paris to-night?"

"A fortunate chance intervened," Immelan replied.

"Fortunate?"

Immelan watched Nigel's retreating figure with a menacing frown.

"I find it so," he replied. "Our wonderful prima donna is in great voice to-night—and I like to be prepared for all possible combinations."

XI

Maggie came suddenly into the library at Belgrave Square, where Jesson, Chalmers and Nigel were talking together. She carried in her hand a note, which she handed to the latter.

"Naida is a dear, after all," she declared. "There is one person at least who does not wish to have me pass away in a German nursing home or fall a victim to Frau Essendorf's cooking."

Nigel read the note aloud. It consisted of only a sentence or two and was dated from the Milan Court that morning:

> Maggie dear, this is just a line of advice from your friend. You must not go back to Germany.
>
> Naida

"I fear," Maggie sighed, "that my little expedition is scotched, even if I had been able to persuade you others to let me go. Every one seems to have made up their mind that I shall not go to Germany. It will be such a disappointment to those flaxen-haired atrocities, Gertrud and Bertha. Their so-much-loved Miss Brown can never return to them again."

"In any case, the game was scarcely worth the candle," Nigel observed. "We have already all the evidence we require that some scheme inimical to this country is being proposed and fostered by Immelan. Our next move must be to find out the nature of this scheme—whether it be naval, military, or political. I don't think Essendorf would be at all likely to give away any more interesting information in the domestic circle."

"What are we all going to do, then?" Maggie asked.

"We are met here to discuss it," Nigel replied. "Jesson is off to Russia this afternoon. I asked him to come round and have a few last words with us, in case there was anything to suggest for us stay-at-homes."

"We shall have to rely very largely upon luck," Jesson declared. "There are three places, in any of which we might discover what we want to know. One is Kroten, another is Paris, provided that Prince Shan really goes there, and the third London."

"London?" Maggie repeated.

"There are two people in London," Jesson declared, "who know everything we are seeking to discover. One is Immelan and the other Naida Karetsky."

E. PHILLIPS OPPENHEIM

"It seems to me," Maggie said, "that if that is so, the place for us is where those two people are. What is the importance of Kroten, Mr. Jesson?"

"Kroten," Jesson replied, "is the second of what I have seen referred to in a private diplomatic report, written in an enemy country, as the three mystery cities of the world. The first one is in Germany, and I have already explored it. I have information, but information which without its sequel is valueless. Kroten is the second. Ten years ago it was a town of eighteen thousand inhabitants. To-day there are at least two hundred thousand people there, and it is growing all the time."

"Say, how can a town of that size," Chalmers enquired, "be termed a mystery city in any sense of the word? Travelling's free in Russia. I guess any one that wanted could take a ticket to Kroten."

"A good many do," Jesson assented calmly, "and some never come back. America and Russia are on friendly terms, yet two men in my branch of the service—good fellows they were, too—started out from Washington for Kroten six months ago. Neither of them has been heard of since; neither ever will be."

"How's it done?" Chalmers asked curiously.

"In the first place," Jesson explained, "the city itself stands at the arm of the river, in a sort of cul-de-sac, with absolutely untraversable mountains on three sides of it. All the roads have to come around the plain and enter from eastwards. There is only one line of railway, so that all the approaches into the city are easily guarded."

"That's all right geographically, of course," Nigel admitted, "but what earthly excuse can any one make for keeping tourists or travellers out of the place if they want to go there?"

"That is perhaps the most ingenious thing of all," Jesson replied. "You know that Russia is now practically a tranquil country, but there are certain bands of the extreme Bolshevistic faction who never gave in to authority and who practically exist in the little-known places by means of marauding expeditions. The mountains about Kroten are supposed to have been infested by these nomadic companies. Whether the outrages set down to them are really committed or not, I don't suppose any one knows, but my point of view is that the presence of these people is absolutely encouraged by the Government, to give them an excuse for the most extraordinary precautions in issuing passports or allowing any one from the outside world to pass into the city. If you get in, I understand you are waited upon by the police within half an hour and have to tell them the story of your past life and your future intentions. After that you are allowed to go about on parole. If you get too inquisitive, you are discovered to be in touch with the robber bands, and—well—that's an end of you."

"A nice, salubrious spot," Nigel murmured.

"It sounds most interesting," Maggie declared. "I think a woman would be less likely to cause suspicion," she added hopefully.

"Utterly out of the question," Jesson pronounced. "Kroten is the one place that must be left in my hands. I know more about the getting there than any of you, and I know the tricks of changing my identity."

"I should rather like to go with you," Nigel confessed.

"Impossible!" was the brief reply.

"Why?"

Jesson smiled.

"To be perfectly frank," he said, "because you are developing an interest in the one person in the world who might give success over into our hands. It is necessary for you to remain where you can encourage that interest."

Nigel was a little staggered.

"My friendship with Mademoiselle Karetsky," he protested, "is scarcely likely to influence her political views."

"I am a somewhat close observer," Jesson continued. "You will not ask me to believe that your conversation with mademoiselle in her box at the Opera last night related all the time to—well, shall we say music?"

"Nigel, you never told me you were at the Opera," Maggie intervened. "What made you go?"

"I think that it was a message from Mademoiselle Karetsky," Jesson suggested quietly.

Nigel smiled.

"Upon my word, I think you're going to be a success, Jesson," he declared. "Perhaps you can tell me what we did talk about?"

"I believe I almost could," was the calm reply. "In any case, I think I see the situation as it exists. Mademoiselle Karetsky is a wonderful woman. She has a great, open mind. To a certain extent, of course, she has seen things from the point of view of Paul Matinsky, Immelan, and that little coterie of Russo-Germans who see a future for both countries only in an alliance of the old-fashioned order. Matinsky, however, has always had his doubts. That is why he sent over here the one person whom he trusted. Presently she will make a report, and the whole issue will remain with her. Immelan knows this and pays her ceaseless court. My impression, however, is that his influence is waning. I believe that to-day he is terrified at the bare reflection of how much Naida Karetsky knows."

"You believe that she does know exactly what is intended?" Nigel asked.

"I am perfectly certain of it," Jesson replied. "If she could be induced to tell us everything, my journey to Kroten might just as well be abandoned. Yet somehow I do not think she will go so far as that. The most that we can hope for is that she will advise Matinsky to reject Immelan's proposals, and that she will perhaps bring some influence to bear in the same direction upon Prince Shan."

"I am inclined to agree with Jesson," Nigel pronounced, "inasmuch as I believe that Mademoiselle Karetsky is disposed to change or modify her views concerning us. You see, after all, this threatened blow against England is purely a private affair of Germany's. There is really no reason why Russia or any other country should be dragged into it. She is the monkey pulling the chestnuts out of the fire for her most dangerous rival."

"Matinsky might be brought to think that way," Chalmers observed, "but they say half the members of his Cabinet are under German influence."

"If Matinsky believed that," Nigel declared, "he is quite strong enough to clear them all out and make a fresh start."

"In the meantime," Maggie interposed, "I should like to know in what way you propose to use poor little me? I am not to go to Germany, the man whom I at one time seriously thought of marrying is told off to engage the attentions of another woman, Mr. Jesson here is going to Kroten, and he doesn't show the slightest inclination to take me with him. Am I to sit here and do nothing?"

"There remains for you the third enterprise," Jesson replied, "one in which, so far as I can see," he continued, with a smile, "you have not the faintest chance of success."

"Tell me what it is, at least?" she begged.

"The conversion of Prince Shan."

Maggie made a little grimace.

"Aren't you trying me a little high?" she murmured.

"Very high indeed," Jesson acknowledged. "Prince Shan, for all his wonderful statesmanship and his grip upon world affairs, is reputed to be almost an anchorite in his daily life. No woman has ever yet been able to boast of having exercised the slightest influence over him. At the same time, he is an extraordinarily human person, and success with him would mean the end of your enemies."

"It sounds a bit of a forlorn hope," Maggie remarked cheerfully, "but I'll do my little best."

"Prince Shan has abandoned his idea of landing at Paris," Jesson continued. "He is coming direct to London. I have to thank Chalmers for that information. Immelan will meet him directly he arrives, and their first conversations will make history. Afterwards, if things go well, Mademoiselle Karetsky will join the conference."

"I fear," Maggie sighed, "that there will be difficulties in the way of my establishing confidential relations with Prince Shan."

"There will be difficulties," Jesson assented, "but the thing is not so impossible as it would be in Paris. Prince Shan has a very fine house in Curzon Street, which is kept in continual readiness for him. He will probably entertain to some extent. You will without doubt have opportunities of meeting him socially."

Maggie glanced at herself in the glass.

"A Chinaman!" she murmured.

"I guess that doesn't mean what it did," Chalmers pointed out. "Prince Shan is an aristocrat and a born ruler. He has every scrap of culture that we know anything about and something from his thousand-year-old family that we don't quite know how to put into words. Don't you worry about Prince Shan, Lady Maggie. Ask Dorminster here what they called him at Oxford."

"The first gentleman of Asia," Nigel replied. "I think he deserves the title."

XII

On the morning following the conclave in Belgrave Square, the Right Honourable Mervin Brown received two extremely distinguished visitors in Downing Street. It was doubtful whether the Prime Minister was altogether at his best. There was a certain amount of irritability rankling beneath his customary air of bonhommie. He motioned his callers to take chairs, however, and listened attentively to the few words of introduction which his secretary thought necessary.

"This is General Dumesnil, sir, of the French Staff, and Monsieur Pouilly of the French Cabinet. They have called according to appointment, on Government business."

"Very glad to see you, gentlemen," was the Prime Minister's brisk welcome. "Sorry I can't talk French to you. Politics, these last ten years, haven't left us much time for the outside graces."

Monsieur Pouilly at once took the floor. He was a thin, dark man with a beautifully trimmed black beard, flashing black eyes, and thoughtful, delicate features. He was attired in the frock coat and dark trousers of diplomatic usage, and he appeared to somewhat resent the brown tweed suit and soft collar of the man who was receiving him.

"Mr. Mervin Brown," he began, "you will kindly look upon our visit as official. We are envoys from Monsieur le Président and the French Government. General Dumesnil has accompanied me, in case our conversation should turn upon military matters here or at the War Office."

The General saluted. The Prime Minister bowed a little awkwardly.

"So far as I am concerned," the latter declared, "I will be perfectly frank with you from the start. I know nothing whatever about military affairs. My job is to govern this country, to make the most of its resources, and to bring prosperity to its citizens from the English Channel to the North Sea. We don't need soldiers and never shall, that I can see. I am firmly convinced that the days of wars are over. The government of every country in the world is getting into the hands of the democracy, and the democracy don't want war and never did. If any of the more quarrelsome folk on the continent get scrapping, well, my conception of my duty is to keep out of it."

Monsieur Pouilly restrained himself. To judge from his appearance, however, it was not altogether an easy matter.

"You belong, sir," he said, "to a type of statesman whose rise to power in this country some of us have watched with a certain amount of concern, for although it is not my mission here to-day to talk politics, I am yet bound to remind you that you do not stand alone. The very League of Nations upon which you rely imposes certain obligations upon you, some actual, some understood. It is to discuss the situation arising from your neglect to make the provisions called for in that agreement that I am here to-day."

Mr. Mervin Brown glanced at some figures which his secretary had laid before him.

"You complain, I presume, of the reduction of our standing army?" he observed.

"We complain of that," Monsieur Pouilly replied, "and we complain also of the gradually decreasing interest shown by your Government in matters of æronautics, artillery, and naval construction. We learnt our lesson in 1914. If trouble should come again, our country would once more be the sufferer. You would no doubt do everything that was expected of you, in time. Before you were ready, however, France would be ruined. You entered into certain obligations under the League of Nations. My Government begs to call your attention to the fact that you are not fulfilling them."

"It is my intention within the course of the next few months," Mervin Brown declared, "to lay before the League of Nations a scheme for total disarmament."

Monsieur Pouilly was staggered. A little exclamation escaped the General.

"What about those nations," the latter enquired, "who were left outside the League? What of Russia, for instance?"

"Russia is a great and peaceful republic," Mervin Brown replied. "All her efforts are devoted towards industrial development. No nation would have less to gain by a return to militarism."

"Pardon, monsieur, but how do you know anything about Russia?" Monsieur Pouilly asked. "You have not a single secret service agent there, and your ambassadors are ambassadors of commerce."

"I know what every one else knows," Mervin Brown declared. "Our commercial travellers are our secret service agents. They travel where they please in Russia."

"And Germany?" the General queried.

"I defy you to say that there is the slightest indication of any militarism in Germany," the Prime Minister insisted. "I was there myself only a few months ago. The country is quiet and moving on now to a new prosperity. I am absolutely and entirely convinced that the world has nothing to fear from either Russia or Germany."

"Have you any theory, sir," General Dumesnil enquired, "as to why Russia refused to join the League of Nations?"

"None whatever," was the genial acknowledgment. "Russia was left out at the start through jealous statesmanship, and afterwards she preferred her independence. I have every sympathy with her attitude."

"One more question," the soldier begged. "Are you aware, sir, that since Japan left the League of Nations on the excuse of her isolation, she has been building æroplanes and battleships on a new theory, instigated, if you please, by China?"

"And look at her last balance sheet as a result of it," was the prompt retort. "If a nation chooses to make herself a bankrupt by building war toys, no one in the world can help her. Legislation of that sort is foolish and simply an incitement to revolution. Look at the difference in our country. Our income tax is practically abolished, our industrial troubles are over. Our credit never stood so high, the wealth of the country was never so great. We are satisfied. A peaceful nation makes for peace. The rattling of the sabre incites military disturbance. Do not ask us, gentlemen, to train armies or build ships."

"We ask you only to keep your covenant," Monsieur Pouilly pronounced stiffly.

"Who does keep it?" the Prime Minister demanded. "The world is governed now by common sense and humanity. I look upon a war of aggression on the part of any country as a sheer impossibility."

"What about a war of revenge?" the General enquired quietly.

"You can search Germany from end to end," Mervin Brown declared, "and find no trace of any spirit of the sort. I am sorry if I am a disappointment to you, gentlemen, but the present Government views your attitude without sympathy. General Richardson is expecting a visit from you this morning at the War Office, and he will give you any information you desire. An appointment has also been made for you this afternoon at the Admiralty. You are doing me the honour of dining with me here to-morrow night to meet certain members of my Cabinet, and we will, if you choose, discuss the matter further then. I have thought it best to place my views clearly before you, however, at the outset of your visit here."

The Frenchmen rose a few minutes later and took their leave, ceremoniously but with obvious discontent. The Prime Minister leaned back in his chair and awaited his secretary's return with a well-satisfied smile. In a few minutes the latter presented himself.

"Well, Franklin," the great man said, "I've let them hear the truth for once. Plain speaking, eh?"

The young man bowed.

"They certainly know your views, sir."

The Minister glanced at his subordinate sharply.

"What's the matter with you this morning, Franklin?" he demanded.

"There is nothing the matter with me, thank you, sir," was the quiet reply.

"You're not going to tell me that you disapprove of my attitude?"

"By no means, sir," the young man assured his Chief hastily,—"not altogether, that is to say. At the same time, one wonders how far those two men represent the feeling of France."

His Chief shrugged his shoulders.

"The military spirit is hard to kill," he said. "It is in the blood of most Frenchmen. They are not big enough to understand that the world is moving on to greater things. What did they say to you before they left?"

"Nothing much, sir. The General just asked me whether I thought you would soon be content to leave London unpoliced."

"What rubbish! Any one else for me to see this morning?"

"You promised to give Lord Dorminster ten minutes," the young man reminded him. "He is in the anteroom now."

The Prime Minister frowned.

"Dorminster," he repeated. "He is a nephew of the man who was always worrying the Government to reëstablish the secret service. I remember he came to see me the other day, declared that his uncle had been murdered, and a secret dispatch from Germany stolen. I wonder he didn't wind up with a report that the Chinese were on their way to seize Ireland!"

"It is the same man, sir."

"Well, I suppose I'd better see him and get it over," his Chief declared irritably. "If only one could make these people realize how far behind the times they are!"

Nigel was shown in, a few minutes later. Mr. Mervin Brown was gracious but terse.

"I haven't had the opportunity of congratulating you upon becoming one of our hereditary legislators, Lord Dorminster, since you took your seat in the House of Lords," he said. "Pray let me do so now. I hope that we may count upon your support."

"My support, sir," Nigel replied, "will be given to any Party which will take the urgent necessary steps to protect this country against a great danger."

"God bless my soul!" the Prime Minister exclaimed. "Another of you!"

"I can only guess who my predecessors were," Nigel continued, smiling, "but I will frankly confess that the object of my visit is to beg you to reëstablish our secret service in Germany, Russia and China."

"Nothing," the other declared, "would induce me to do anything of the sort."

"Are you aware," Nigel enquired, "that there is a considerable foreign secret service at work in this country at the present moment?"

"I am not aware of it, and I don't believe it," was the blunt retort.

"I have absolute proof," Nigel insisted. "Not only that, but two ex-secret service men whom my uncle sent out to Germany and Russia on his own account were murdered there as soon as they began to get on the track of certain things which had been kept secret. A report from one of these men got through and was stolen from my uncle's library in Belgrave Square on the day he was murdered. You will remember that I placed all these facts before you on the occasion of a previous visit."

Mervin Brown nodded.

"Anything else?" he asked patiently.

"You know that a special envoy from China is on his way here at the present moment to meet Immelan?"

"Oscar Immelan, the German Commissioner?"

"The same," Nigel assented.

"A most delightful fellow," the Prime Minister declared warmly, "and a great friend to this country."

"I must take the liberty of disagreeing with you," Nigel rejoined, "because I know very well that he is our bitter enemy. Prince Shan, who is on his way from China to meet him, is the envoy of the one country outside Europe whom we might fear. We sit still and do nothing. We have no means of knowing what may be plotted against us here in London. At least a polite request might be sent to Prince Shan to ask him to pay you a visit and disclose the nature of his conference with Immelan."

"If he cares to come, we shall be glad to see him," Mervin Brown replied, "but I for one shall not go out of my way to talk politics."

"Do you know what politics are, sir?" Nigel asked, in a sudden fury.

The Prime Minister's eyes flashed for a moment. He controlled himself, however, and rang the bell.

"I have an idea that I do," he answered. "A few millions of my fellow countrymen believe the same thing, or I should not be here. I think that you know what my principles are, Lord Dorminster. I am here to govern this country for the benefit of the people. We don't want to govern any one else's country, we don't want to meddle in any one else's affairs. Least of all do we want to revert to the times when your uncle was a young man, and every country in Europe was sitting with drawn sword, trusting nobody, fearing everybody, living in a state of nerves, with the roll of the drum always in their ears. The best preventative of war, in my opinion, is not to believe in it. Good morning, Lord Dorminster."

It was a dismissal against which there was no appeal. Nigel followed the secretary from the room.

"You found the Chief a little bit ratty this morning, I expect, Lord Dorminster," the latter remarked. "We've had the French Mission here."

"Mr. Mervin Brown has at least the virtue of knowing his own mind," Nigel replied dryly.

XIII

The automobile turned in through the great entrance gates of the South London Aeronautic Terminus and commenced a slow ascent along the broad asphalted road to what, a few years ago, had been esteemed a new wonder of the world. Maggie rose to her feet with a little exclamation of wonder.

"Do you know I have never been here at night before?" she exclaimed. "Isn't it wonderful!"

"Marvellous!" Nigel replied. "It's the largest aeronautic station in the world—bigger, they say, than all our railway termini put together. Look at the flares, Maggie! No wonder the sky from the housetop at Belgrave Square seems always to be on fire at night!"

They were approaching now the first of the huge sheds which were arranged in circular fashion around an immense stretch of perfectly level asphalted ground. Every shed was as big as an ordinary railway station, its arched opening framed with electric illuminations. Inside could be seen the crowds of people waiting on the platforms; in many of them, the engine of a great airship was already throbbing, waiting to start. In the background was a huge wireless installation, and around, at regular intervals, enormous pillars, on the top of which flares of different-coloured fire were burning. The automobile came to a standstill before a large electrically illuminated time chart. Nigel alighted for a moment and spoke to one of the inspectors.

"Which station for the *Black Dragon*, private ship from China?" he enquired.

The man glanced at the chart.

"Number seven, on the other side," he replied. "You can drive around."

"How is she for time?"

"She crossed the North Sea punctually," he replied. "We should see her violet lights in ten minutes. Mind the traffic as you pass number three. The North ship from Norway is just in."

Nigel addressed a word of caution to the chauffeur, and they drove on. From the first shed they passed a stream of vehicles was pouring out,—porters with luggage, jostling throngs of newly arrived passengers on their way to the Electric Underground. They drove into number seven shed, left the car, and walked to the end of the long platform. The great arc of glass-covered roof above them was brilliantly illuminated, throwing a queer downward light upon the long line of waiting porters, the refreshment rooms, the kiosks and newspaper stalls. In the far end, a huge airship, bound for the East, was already filling up. Maggie and her companion stood for a few minutes gazing into the huge void of space.

"Tell me about Naida," the former begged, a little abruptly.

"Naida is a wonderful woman," Nigel declared enthusiastically. "We lunched at Ciro's. She wore a black and white muslin gown which arrived this morning from Paris. Afterwards we went down to Ranelagh and sat under the trees."

"Throwing yourself thoroughly into your little job, aren't you!" Maggie sniffed.

"You'll have a chance to catch me up before long," he replied. "Naida has promised that she will arrange a meeting with the Prince."

"I wonder what Oscar Immelan will have to say about it," Maggie reflected.

"To tell you the truth," Nigel said hopefully, "I believe that Immelan is losing ground. His whole scheme is too selfish. Of course, Naida won't discuss these things with me in plain words, but she gives me a hint now and then. Amongst her gifts, she has a marvellous sense of justice and a hatred of any form of bribery. That is where I feel convinced that she and Immelan will never come together. Immelan could never see more than the selfish side, even of a world upheaval. Naida searches everywhere for motive. She has the altruistic instinct. I wonder no longer at Matinsky. She is a born ruler herself."

"I'm glad you are getting along with her," Maggie remarked. "Look!" she broke off, catching at his arm. "The violet lights!"

High up in the sky outside, two violet specks of light suddenly rose and fell like airballs. A crowd of mechanics appeared through subterranean doors and stood about in the vast arena. Very soon the airship came into sight, her cars brilliantly illuminated. She circled slowly round and came noiselessly to the ground, and with the mechanics running by her side, and her engines now scarcely audible, came slowly into the shed and to a standstill by the side of the platform. Maggie and her companion stood well in the background.

"There he is," the latter whispered.

Immelan, suddenly appeared as though from the bowels of the earth, was shaking hands warmly with a tall, slender man who was one of the first to descend from the airship. They talked rapidly together for a few minutes. Then they disappeared, walking down towards the luggage-clearing station. Maggie watched the retreating figures earnestly.

"He doesn't look in the least Chinese," she declared.

"I told you he didn't," Nigel replied. "He was considered the best-looking man of his year up at Oxford."

Maggie was unusually silent on their way back.

"It was perhaps scarcely worth our while, this little expedition of ours," Maggie said thoughtfully.

"You're not sorry that we came?" he asked.

She shook her head. "I think not," she replied.

"Why only 'think'?"

She roused herself with an effort.

"I don't know, Nigel," she confessed. "I can't imagine what is wrong with me. I feel shivery—nervous—as though something were going to happen."

He looked at her curiously. This was a Maggie whom he scarcely recognised.

"Presentiments?" he asked.

"Absurd, isn't it!" she replied, with a weak smile. "I'll get over it directly. I don't think I am going to like Prince Shan, Nigel."

"Well, you haven't been long making up your mind," he observed. "I shouldn't have thought you had been able even to see his face."

"I had a queer, lightning-like glimpse of it," she reflected. "To me it seemed as though it were carved out of granite, and as though all that was human about him were the mouth and the eyes. I wish he hadn't been looking."

"Are you flattering yourself that he will recognise you?" Nigel asked.

"I know that he will," she answered simply.

IN A CORNER OF THE white-and-gold restaurant at the Ritz on the following evening, Prince Shan and Immelan dined tête-à-tête, Immelan in the best of spirits, talking of the pleasant trifles of the world, drinking champagne and pointing out notabilities; Prince Shan, his features and expression unchanging, and his face as white as the perfectly fitting shirt he wore. His clothes were fashionable and distinctive, his black pearls unobtrusive but wonderful, his smoothly brushed dark hair, his immaculate finger nails, his skilfully tied tie all indicative of his close touch with western civilization. There was nothing, in fact, except his sphinx-like expression, the slightly unusual shape of his brilliant eyes, and his queer air of personal detachment, to denote the Oriental. He drank water, he ate sparingly, he preserved an almost unbroken silence, yet he had the air of one giving courteous attention to everything which his companion said and finding interest in it. Only once he asked a question.

"You are well acquainted here, my host," he said. "You know the trio at the table just behind the entrance—the attractive young lady with her chaperon, and a gentleman who I rather fancy must be an old college acquaintance whose name I have forgotten. Tell me some more about them in their private capacity, and not as saviours of their country."

Immelan frowned slightly as he glanced across the room.

"There is not much to tell," he answered, without enthusiasm. "The young lady is, as you know, Lady Maggie Trent. The older lady, with the white hair, is, I believe, her aunt. The name of their escort is Lord Dorminster. You would probably know him by the name of Kingley— he has only just succeeded to the title."

Prince Shan was looking straight across the room, his eyes travelling over the heads of the many brilliant little groups of diners to rest apparently upon an empty space in the white-and-gold walls. He had been a great traveller, but always his first evening, when he came once more into touch with a civilisation more meretricious but more poignant than his own, resulted in this disturbing cloud of sensations. His companion's voice sounded emptily in his ears.

"They say that the young lady is engaged to Lord Dorminster. That is only gossip, however."

For the second time Prince Shan looked directly at the little group. His eyes rested upon Maggie, simply dressed but wonderfully *soignée*, very alluring, laughing up into the face of her escort. Their eyes did not actually meet, but each was conscious of the other's regard. Once more he felt the disturbance of the West.

"If we should chance to come together naturally," he said, "it would gratify me to make the acquaintance of Lady Maggie Trent."

XIV

The introduction which Prince Shan had requested came about very naturally. The lounge of the hotel was more than usually crowded that evening, and the table towards which an attentive *maître d'hôtel* conducted Immelan and his companion was next to the one reserved by Nigel. The transference of a chair opened up conversation. Immelan was bland and ingenuous as usual, introducing every one, glad, apparently, to make one common party. Prince Shan remained by Maggie's side after the introduction had been effected. A chair which Immelan schemed to offer him elsewhere he calmly refused.

"This is my first evening in London, Lady Maggie," he said. "I am fortunate."

"Why?" she asked.

He looked at her meditatively. Then he accepted her unspoken invitation and seated himself on the lounge by her side.

"We who come from the self-contained countries of the world," he explained, "and China is one of them, come always with the desire and longing for new experiences, new sensations. My own appetite for these is insatiable."

"And am I a new sensation?" Maggie asked, glancing up at him innocently enough, but with a faint gleam of mockery in her eyes.

"You are," he answered placidly. "You reveal—or rather you suggest—the things of which in my country we know nothing."

"But I thought you were all so hyper-civilised over there," Maggie observed. "Please tell me at once what it is that I possess which your womenkind do not."

"If I answered all that your question implies," he said, "I should make use of speech too direct for the conventions of the world in which you live. I would simply remind you that whereas we men in China may claim, I think, to have reached the same standard of culture and civilisation as Europeans, we have left our womenkind far behind in that respect. The Chinese woman, even the noble lady, does not care for serious affairs. The God of the Mountains, as they call him, made her a flower to pluck, a beautiful plaything for her chosen mate. She remains primitive. That is why, in time, man wearies of her, why the person of imagination looks sometimes westward, finds a new joy and a strange new fascination in a wholly different type of femininity."

"But you have many European women now living in China," Maggie reminded him,—"American women, too, and they are so much admired everywhere."

"The Chinese, especially we of the nobility," Prince Shan replied, "are born with racial prejudices. An individual may forgive an affront, a nation never. The days of retaliation by force of arms may indeed have passed, but the gentleman of China, even of these days, is not likely to take to his heart the woman of America."

"Dear me," Maggie murmured, "isn't it rather out of date to persevere in these ancient feuds?"

"Feeling of all sorts is out of date," he admitted patiently, "yet there are some things which endure. I should be honoured by your friendship, Lady Maggie."

"This is very sudden," she laughed. "I am very flattered—but what does it mean?"

"Permission to call upon you—and your aunt," he added, glancing around the little circle.

"We shall be delighted," Maggie replied, "but you won't like my aunt. She is a little deaf, and she has no sense of humour. She has come to live with us because Lord Dorminster and I are not really related, although we call ourselves cousins, and I should hate to leave Belgrave Square. You shall take me out to tea to-morrow afternoon instead, if you like."

A smouldering fire burned for a moment in his eyes.

"That will make me very happy," he said. "I shall attend you at four o'clock."

Thenceforward, conversation became general. Prince Shan, with the air of one who has achieved his immediate object, left his place by Maggie's side and talked with grave courtesy to her aunt. Presently the little party broke up, bound, it seemed, for the same theatre. Nigel had become a little serious.

"Well, you've made a good start, Maggie," he remarked, leaning forward in his place in the limousine.

"Have I?" Maggie answered thoughtfully. "I wonder!"

"I wish we could get at him in some different fashion," her companion observed uneasily.

"My dear man, I'm hardened to these enterprises," Maggie assured him. "I even let the President of the German Republic hold my hand once when his wife wasn't looking. Nothing came of it," she added, with a little sigh. "These Germans are terribly sentimental when it doesn't cost them anything. They've no idea of a fair exchange."

"By a 'fair exchange' you mean," her aunt suggested, a little censoriously, "that you expected him to barter his country's secrets for a touch of your fingers?"

"Or my lips, perhaps," Maggie added, with a little grimace. "Please don't look so serious, Aunt. I'm not really in love with Prince Shan, you know, and to-night I rather feel like marrying Nigel, if I can get him back again. I like his waistcoat buttons, and the way he has tied his tie."

"Too late, my dear," Nigel warned her. "I give you formal notice. I have transferred my affections."

"That decides me," Maggie declared firmly. "I shall collect you back again. I hate to lose an admirer."

"The nonsense you young people talk!" Mrs. Bollington Smith observed, as they reached the theatre.

Chalmers joined them soon after they had reached their box. He sank into the empty place by Maggie's side which Nigel had just vacated and leaned forward confidentially.

"So you've started the campaign," he whispered.

"How do you know?" she enquired.

"I was at the Ritz to-night," he told her, "at the far end of the room with my Chief and two other men. We were behind you in the lounge afterwards."

"I was so engrossed," Maggie murmured.

Chalmers paused for a moment to watch the performance. When he spoke again, his voice, was, for him, unusually serious.

"Young lady," he said, "I told you on our first meeting my idea of diplomacy. Truth! No beating about the bush—just the plain, unvarnished truth! I have conceived an affection for you."

"Goodness gracious!" Maggie exclaimed softly. "Are you going to propose?"

"Nothing," he assured her, "is farther from my thoughts. Lest I should be misunderstood, let me substitute the term 'affectionate interest' for 'affection.' I have felt uneasy ever since I saw Prince Shan watching you across the restaurant to-night."

"Did he really watch me?" Maggie asked complacently.

"He not only watched you," Chalmers assured her, "but he thought about you—and very little else."

"Congratulate me, then," she replied. "I am on the way to success."

Chalmers frowned.

"I'm not quite so sure," he said. "You'll think I'm an illogical sort of person, but I've changed my mind about your rôle in this little affair."

"Why?"

"Because I am afraid of Prince Shan," he answered deliberately.

She looked at him from behind her fan. Her eyes sparkled with interest. If there were any other feeling underneath, she showed no trace of it.

"What a queer word for you to use!"

He nodded.

"I know it. I would back you, Lady Maggie, to hold your own against any male creature breathing, of your own order and your own race, but Prince Shan plays the game differently. He possesses every gift which women and men both admire, but he hasn't our standards. Life for him means power. A wish for him entails its fulfilment."

"You are afraid," Maggie suggested, still with the laughter in her eyes, "that he will trifle with my affections?"

"Something like that," he admitted bluntly. "Prince Shan will be here for a week—perhaps a fortnight. When he goes, he goes a very long distance away."

"I may decide to marry him," Maggie said. "One gets rather tired here of the regular St. George's, Hanover Square, business, and all that comes afterwards."

"Dear Lady Maggie," Chalmers replied, "that is the trouble. Prince Shan would never marry you."

"Why not?" she asked simply.

"First of all," Chalmers went on, after a moment's hesitation, "because Prince Shan, broad-minded though he seems to be and is on all the great questions of the world, still preserves something of what we should call the superstition of his country and order. I believe, in his own mind, he looks upon himself as being one of the few elect of the earth. He travels, he is gracious everywhere, but though his manner is the perfection of form, in his heart he is still aloof. He rides through the clouds from Asia, and he leaves always something of himself over there on the other side. Let me tell you this, Lady Maggie. I have never forgotten it. He was at Harvard in my year, and so far as he unbent to any one, he sometimes unbent to me. I asked him once whether he were ever going to marry. He shook his head and sighed. 'I can never marry,' he replied. 'Why not?' I asked him. 'Because there are no women of the Shan line alive,' he answered. Later, he took pity on my bewilderment. He let me understand. For two thousand years, no Shan has married, save one of his own line. To ally himself with a princess of the royal house of England would be a mésalliance which would disturb his ancestors in their graves. Of course, this sounds to us very ridiculous, but to him it isn't. It is part of the religion of his life."

"You are not very encouraging, are you?" Maggie remarked. "Perhaps he has changed since those days."

Her companion shook his head.

"I should say not," he replied, "the Prince is not of the order of those who change."

"Is it matrimony alone," she asked, "which he denies himself?"

Chalmers glanced towards Mrs. Bollington Smith, whose eyes were closed. Then he nodded towards the stage.

"You see the woman who has just come upon the stage?"

Maggie glanced downwards. A very wonderful little figure in white satin, lithe and sinuous as a cat, Chinese in the subtlety of her looks, European in her almost sinister over-civilisation, stood smiling blandly at the applauding audience.

"La Belle Nita," Maggie murmured. "I thought she was in Paris. Well, what of her?"

"She is reputed to be a protégée of Prince Shan. You see how she looks up at his box."

Maggie was conscious of a queer and almost incomprehensible stab at the heart. She answered without hesitation or change of expression, however.

"The Prince must be kind to a fellow countrywoman," she declared indulgently. "You are talking terrible scandal."

La Belle Nita danced wonderfully, sang like a linnet, danced again and disappeared, notwithstanding the almost wild calls for an encore. With the end of her turn came a selection from the orchestra and a general emptying of the boxes. Presently Chalmers went in search of Nigel. A few moments later there was a knock at the door. Maggie gripped the sides of her chair tightly. She was moved almost to fury by the turmoil in which she found herself. Her invitation to enter was almost inaudible.

"I am deserted," Prince Shan explained, as he made his bow and took the chair to which Maggie pointed. "My friend Immelan has left me to visit acquaintances, and I chance to be unattended this evening. I trust that I do not intrude."

"You are very welcome here," Maggie replied. "Will you listen to the orchestra, or talk to me?"

"I will talk, if I may," he answered. "Lord Dorminster is not with you?"

"Nigel went to look up a friend whom he wants to bring to supper. He is one of those people who seem to discover friends and acquaintances in every quarter of the globe."

"And to that fortunate chance," her visitor continued, dropping his voice a little, "I owe the happiness of finding you alone."

Maggie glanced towards her aunt, who was leaning back in her seat.

"Aunt seems to be asleep, but she isn't," she declared. "She is really a very efficient chaperon. Talk to me about China, please, and tell me about your *Dragon* airship. Is it true that you have silver baths, and that Gauteron painted the walls of your dining salon?"

"One is in the air five days on the way over," he answered indifferently. "It is necessary that one's surroundings should be agreeable. Perhaps some day I may have the honour of showing it to you. In the darkness, and when she is docked, there is little to be seen."

She looked at him curiously.

"You knew that I was there, then?"

"Yours was the first face I saw when I descended from the car," he told her. "You stood apart, watching, and I wondered why. I knew, too, that you would be at the Ritz to-night. That is why I came there. As a rule, I do not dine in public."

"How could you possibly know that I was going to be there?" Maggie asked curiously.

"I sent a gentleman of my suite to look through the names of those who had booked tables," he answered. "It was very simple."

"It was only a chance that the table was reserved in my name," she reminded him.

"It was chance which brought us together," he rejoined. "It is chance under another name to which I trust in life."

For the first time in her life, in her relations with the other sex, Maggie felt a queer sensation which was almost fear. She felt herself losing poise, her will governed, her whole self dominated. Unconsciously she drew herself a little away. Her eyes travelled around the crowded house and suddenly rested on the box which her visitor had just vacated.

Seated behind the curtains, but leaning slightly forward, her eyes fixed intently upon Prince Shan, was La Belle Nita, a green opera cloak thrown around her dancing costume, a curious, striking little figure in the semi-obscurity.

"You have some one waiting for you in your box," Maggie told him.

He glanced across the auditorium and rose to his feet. She gave him credit for the adroitness of mind which rejected the obvious explanation of her presence there.

"I must go," he said simply, "but I have many things which I desire to say to you. You will not forget to-morrow afternoon?"

"I shall not forget," she answered, in a low tone.

XV

There was a half reluctant admiration in Prince Shan's eyes as he sat back in the dim recesses of his box and scrutinised his visitor. La Belle Nita had learnt all that Paris and London could teach her.

"You are very beautiful, Nita," he said.

"Many men tell me so," she answered.

"Life has gone well with you since we met last?" he asked reflectively.

"The months have passed," she replied.

"You have been faithful?"

"Fidelity is of the soul."

He paused, as though pondering over her answer. A famous French comedian was holding the stage, and the house rocked with laughter.

"You have the same apartment?"

She pressed the clasp of a black velvet bag which rested on the edge of the box, opened it, and passed him a key.

"It is the same."

He held the key in his fingers for a moment, but he had the air of a man to whom the action had no significance.

"You have enough money?" he asked.

"I have saved a million francs," she told him. "I am waiting for my lord to speak of things that matter. The woman in the box over there—who is she?"

"An English spy," he answered calmly.

She lowered her eyes for a moment, as though to conceal the sudden soft flash.

"An English spy," she repeated. "My rival in espionage."

"You have no rival, Nita," he replied, "and she is in the opposite camp."

Her two red lips were distorted into a pout.

"Is it over, my task?" she asked. "I am weary of Paris. I love it over here better. I am weary of French officers, of these solemn officials who come to my room like guilty schoolboys, and who speak of themselves and their importance with bated breath, as though their whisper would rock the world. My master has enough information?"

"More than enough," he assured her. "You have done your work wonderfully."

"Shall I now deal with her?" she continued, with a slight, eager movement of her head towards the opposite box.

He smiled.

"She is harmless, she and her entourage," he replied. "Some stroke of good fortune brought them word of the meeting between myself and Immelan, and beyond that they guessed at its significance. They were at the shed to watch my arrival. Now, with their mouths open, they sit and wait for the information which they hope will drop in. They are very ingenuous, these Anglo-Saxons, but they are not diplomats."

She turned her head and looked across the auditorium. Maggie was talking to a man whom Nigel had just brought in, and who was bending over her in obvious admiration. Nita, with her wealth of cosmetics, her over-red lips, stared curiously at this possible rival, with her clear skin, her beautiful neck and shoulders, her hair dressed close to her head, her air of quiet, almost singular distinction.

"The young lady," she confessed, "wears her clothes well for an English woman. She is *bien soignée*, but she looks a little difficult."

His eyes followed the direction of hers, and her object was achieved. She read correctly the light that gleamed in them.

"I may come to-night?" she asked quietly.

He shook his head.

"Not again," he replied.

A violinist now held the stage, a Pole newly come to London. La Belle Nita closed her eyes. For a few minutes her sorrow seemed to throb to the minor music to which she was listening.

"For all my work, then," she said presently, "for the suffering and the risk, there is to be nothing?"

"Is it nothing for you to be invited to live in whatsoever manner you choose?" he remonstrated.

"It is little," she replied steadily. "There are a dozen who would do this for me, who pray every day that they may do so. What are all these things beside the love of my master?"

He looked at her a little sadly, yet without any sign of real feeling. To him she represented nothing more than a doll with brains, from whose intelligence he had profited, but of whose beauty he was weary.

"You know what our poet says, Nita," he reminded her. "'Love is like the rustling of the wind in the almond trees before dawn.' We cannot command it. It comes to us or leaves us without reason."

She looked across the auditorium once more and spoke with her head turned away from her companion.

"There is no one in the East," she said, "because those who write me weekly send news of my lord's doings. There is no one in the East, because there they give the body who know nothing of the soul. And so my Prince is safe amongst them. But here—these western women have other gifts. Is that she, master of my life and soul?"

"I met her this evening for the first time," he replied.

She laughed drearily.

"Eyes may meet in the street without speech, a glance may burn its way into the soul. Once I thought that I might love again, because a stranger smiled at me in the Bois, and he had grey eyes, and that look about his mouth which a woman craves for. He passed on, and I forgot. You see, my lord was still there.—So this is the woman."

"Who knows?" he answered.

Immelan came into the box a little abruptly. There was a cloud upon his face which he did his best to conceal. Almost simultaneously, a messenger from behind the scenes arrived for Nita. She rose to her feet and wrapped her green cloak closely around her lissom figure.

"In a quarter of an hour," she said, "I have to appear again. It is to be good-night, then?"

She raised her eyes to his, and for a moment the appeal which knows no nationality shone out of their velvety depths. She stood before him simply, like a slave who pleads. Not a muscle of Prince Shan's face moved.

"It is to be good-night, Nita," he answered calmly.

Her head drooped, and she passed out. She had the air of a flower whose petals have been bruised. Immelan looked after her curiously, almost compassionately.

"It is finished, then, with the little one, Prince?" he enquired.

"It is finished," was the calm reply.

Immelan stroked his short moustache thoughtfully.

"Is it wise?" he ventured. "She has been faithful and assiduous. She knows many things."

Prince Shan's eyes were filled with mild wonder.

"She has had some years of my occasional companionship," he said. "It is surely as much as she could hope for or expect. We are not like you Westerners, Immelan," he went on. "Our women are the creatures of our will. We call them, or we send them away. They know that, and they are prepared."

"It seems a little brutal," Immelan muttered.

"You prefer your method?" his companion asked. "Yet you practise deceit. Your fancy wanders, and you lie about it. You lose your dignity, my friend. No woman is worth a man's lie."

Immelan was leaning back in his chair, gazing steadfastly across the crowded theatre.

"Your principles," he said, "are suited to your own womenkind. La Belle Nita has become westernised. Are you sure that she accepts the situation as she would if she dwelt with you in Pekin?"

"I am her master," Prince Shan declared calmly. "I have made no promises that I have not fulfilled."

"The promise between a man and a woman is an unspoken one," Immelan persisted. "You have not been in Europe for five months. All that time she has awaited you."

"Something else has happened," Prince Shan said deliberately.

"Since your arrival in London?"

"Since my arrival in London, since I stepped out of my ship last night."

Immelan was frankly incredulous.

"You mean Lady Maggie Trent?"

"Certainly! I have always felt that some day or other my thoughts would turn towards one of these strange, western women. That time has come. Lady Maggie possesses those charms which come from the brain, yet which appeal more deeply than any other to the subtle desires of the poet, the man of letters and the philosopher. She is very wonderful, Immelan. I thank you for your introduction."

Immelan ceased to caress his moustache. He leaned back in his chair and gazed at his companion. For many years he and the Prince had been associates, yet at that moment he felt that he had not even begun to understand him.

"But you forget, Prince," he said, "that Lady Maggie and her friends are in the opposite camp. When our agreement is concluded and known to the world, she will look upon you as an enemy."

"As yet," Prince Shan answered calmly, "our agreement is not concluded."

Immelan's face darkened. Nothing but his awe of the man with whom he sat prevented an expression of anger.

"But, Prince," he expostulated, "apart from political considerations, you cannot really imagine that anything would be possible between you and Lady Maggie?"

"Why not?" was the cool reply.

"Lady Maggie is of the English nobility," Immelan pointed out. "Neither she nor her friends would be in the least likely to consider anything in the nature of a morganatic alliance."

"It would not be necessary," Prince Shan declared. "It is in my mind to offer her marriage."

Immelan dropped the cigarette case which he had just drawn from his pocket. He gazed at his companion in blank and unaffected astonishment.

"Marriage?" he muttered. "You are not serious!"

"I am entirely serious," the Prince insisted. "I can understand your amazement, Immelan. When the idea first came into my mind, I tore at it as I would at a weed. But we who have studied in the West have learnt certain great truths which our own philosophers have sometimes missed. All that is best of life and of death our own prophets have taught us. From them we have learnt fortitude and chastity: devotion to our country and singleness of purpose. Over here, though, one has also learnt something. Nobility is of the soul. A Prince of the Shans must seek not for the body but for the spirit of the woman who shall be his mate. If their spirits meet on equal terms, then she may even share the throne of his life."

Immelan was speechless. There was something final and convincing in his companion's measured words. His own protest, when at last he spoke, sounded paltry.

"But supposing it is true that she is already engaged to Lord Dorminster?"

Prince Shan smiled very quietly.

"That," he said, "can easily be disposed of."

"But do you seriously believe that you would be able to induce her to return with you to Pekin?" Immelan persisted.

At that moment it chanced that Maggie turned her head and looked across at the two men. Prince Shan leaned a little forward to meet her gaze. His face was expressionless. The lines of his mouth were calm and restful, yet in his eyes there glowed for a single moment the fire of a man who looks upon the thing he covets.

"I seriously believe it," he answered under his breath.

XVI

M aggie leaned back in her chair with a little sigh of content. The scarlet-coated waiter had just removed their tea tray, a pleasant breeze was rustling through the leaves of the trees under which she and Prince Shan were seated. From the distance came the low strains of a military band. Everywhere on the lawns and along the paths men and women were promenading.

"Confess that this is better than Rumpelmayer's or the Ritz," she murmured lazily.

"It is better," he admitted. "It is a very wonderful place."

"You have nothing like it in China?" she asked him.

"It would not be possible," he answered. "Democracy there is confined to politics. In other respects, our class prejudices are far more rigid than yours. But then I see a great change in this country since I was here as a student."

"You have lost your affection for it, perhaps?" she ventured, looking at him through half-closed eyes.

"On the contrary," he assured her, "my gratitude towards her was never so great as at this moment. Your country has given me nothing I prize so much, Lady Maggie, as my knowledge of you."

She looked away from his very earnest eyes, and the light retort died away upon her lips. The men and women whom she watched so steadfastly seemed like puppets, the flowers artificial, the music unreal. Already she was beginning to resent the influence which he was establishing over her. The art of badinage in which she was so proficient stood her in no stead. Words, even the power of light speech, had deserted her.

"Tell me about the changes that you see," she asked.

"Perhaps," he replied, after a moment's hesitation, "it is because I am an occasional visitor that differences seem so marked to me, but look at the tables there. That is the Duke of Illinton, is it not? At the next table, the man in the strange clothes and uncomfortable hat—it seems to me that I have seen him somewhere under different circumstances."

Maggie nodded.

"Life is a terrible hotchpotch nowadays," she admitted. "After the war, our gentry and aristocracy who were not wealthy were taxed out of existence. The profiteers, and the men who had made fortunes during the war, took their place. It has made the country prosperous but less picturesque."

"You put things very clearly," he said. "To-day in England is certainly the day of the shopkeeper's triumph. Wealth is a great thing, but it is great only for what it leads to. I think your philosopher of the streets, your new school of politicians, have alike forgotten that."

"You have lost sympathy with England, have you not, Prince Shan?" Maggie asked him.

He turned towards her, a faint but kindly smile upon his lips, a light in his eyes which she did not altogether understand.

"Lady Maggie," he said quietly, "they tell me that you are interested in the political side of my visit to this country."

"Who tells you that?" she demanded. "What have I to do with politics?"

"You have been gifted with great intelligence," he continued, "and you are the confidante of your connection, Lord Dorminster. Lord Dorminster is one of those few Englishmen who realise the ill direction of the destinies of this country. You would like to help him in his present very strenuous efforts to ascertain the truth as to certain movements directed against the British Empire. That is so, is it not?"

"In plain words, you are accusing me of being a spy."

"Ah, no!" he protested gently. "No one can be a spy in one's own country. You are within your rights as a patriot in seeking to discover whatever may be useful knowledge to the English Government. That, I fear, is one reason for your kindness to me, Lady Maggie. I trust that it is not the only reason."

She knew better than to make the mistake of denial. After all, it was an absurdly unequal contest.

"It is not the only reason," she assured him, a little tremulously.

"I am glad. One word more upon this subject, and we speak of other things. Please, Lady Maggie, do not stoop to be hopelessly obvious in these efforts of yours. If I drop a pocketbook, believe me there will be nothing in it to interest you. If I speak with Immelan or any other, save in the secrecy of my chamber, there will be nothing which it will be worth your while to overhear. If Lord Dorminster should decide to adopt buccaneering expedients and kidnap me, the attempt would probably fail; and if it succeeded, it would in the end profit you nothing. As you say over here, for your sake, Lady Maggie, I will lay the cards upon the table. I am discussing with Oscar Immelan, and indirectly with an emissary from Russia, a certain scheme which, if carried out, would certainly be harmful to this country. I shall decide for or against that scheme entirely as it seems to me that it will be for the good or evil of my own country. Nothing will change my purpose in that. In your heart you know that nothing should change it. But I bring to the deliberations upon which we are engaged a new sentiment towards your country, since I have known you. Other things being equal, I shall decline the scheme for your sake, Lady Maggie."

There was a curious quivering at the corners of her mouth and a lump in her throat. She was absolutely incapable of speech. His grave and reasonable words seemed to fill her with a sense of importance. Her little efforts and schemes seemed puny, almost laughable.

"So you see," he continued, after a moment's pause, "that you have done your work. You have done it very effectually. You have created a strong sentiment in my mind in favour of this country, a sentiment which I did not previously possess. There is no other way in which you could have influenced the decision soon to be arrived at. In return for what I have told you, Lady Maggie, I ask for no promise, but I beg you to forget the role you played in Germany; not to attempt—you will not be offended?—to influence events so far as I am concerned by any attempt at spying upon my actions, or by treating me any other way than with your whole confidence. I do not ask for any promise. I have said something to you which has been on my mind. Now I shall ask you a favour," he declared, rising to his feet. "You will walk with me through the flower gardens yonder. If there is one thing I miss in this country so much that the want of it makes me sometimes a little homesick," he went on, as they moved away together, "it is the perfume of the flowers in the morning and at night from the gardens of my summer palace. Next time you honour me with an hour or so of your time, I shall ask you to let me bring some pictures of my favourite home in China."

Maggie walked dutifully by his side, answering his frequent questions about flowers and shrubs, listening while he told her about his white peacocks and the tame birds which were his own pets. Suddenly she broke into a fit of laughter. She looked up into his grave face, her eyes imploring him for sympathy.

"I feel so like a precocious child," she exclaimed, "who has been put in her place! No one has ever turned me inside out so skilfully, has made me feel such an ignorant little donkey. Do you know, I half like you for it, Prince Shan, and half detest you."

He seemed suddenly to become younger, to meet her upon her own ground.

"Please do not be angry," he begged. "Please do not think that I look upon you at all as a little child. You have brought something into my life for which I have searched and hoped, and I am deeply grateful to you. Shall I—go on?"

She caught at his wrist.

"Please not," she begged breathlessly. "Be content with this moment."

They had paused by the side of an arbour. She suddenly felt the pressure of his fingers upon her hand.

"I shall be content," he said, in a low tone, the passion of which seemed to throw her senses into complete turmoil, "only when I have what my heart desires. But I will wait."

They walked almost into the midst of a little crowd of acquaintances. Maggie was herself again immediately. She chattered away with Chalmers, and led him off to see a wonderful yellow rose. He watched her curiously. When they found themselves isolated at the end of the garden path, he ignored for a moment their mission.

"Any luck, Lady Maggie?" he asked.

She looked up at him, and to his amazement her eyes were swimming.

"I think that Prince Shan will be on our side," she replied.

XVII

Monsieur Felix Senn, the distinguished Frenchman who had just acquitted himself of the special mission which had brought him to London, was a little loath to depart from the historical chamber in Downing Street. Diplomatically, the interview was over. The Prime Minister, however, on this occasion, was courteous, even affable. There seemed no reason for his visitor to hurry away.

"You will accept, I trust, sir," the latter begged, "this assurance of my extreme regret at the present unfortunate condition of affairs. I am one of those who threw his hat into the air on the boulevards in August, 1914, when the news came that your great country had decided to fulfil her unwritten promises and in the cause of honour had declared war against Germany. I have never forgotten that moment, sir, even in those months and years of misunderstandings which followed the signing of the Treaty of Peace. I was one of those who pointed always to the sacrifices which Great Britain had made on our behalf, to her glorious deeds on land and sea. I have always been a friend of your country, Mr. Mervin Brown. That is why I think I was chosen to bring this dispatch."

"You are very welcome," the Prime Minister assured him. "As for the purpose of your mission, I assure you that I view it less seriously than you do. Glance with me at the position for a moment. Notwithstanding the era of peace which has sprung up all over the world, owing to the happy influence of the League of Nations, France alone has decided to follow still the path of militarism. Your last year's army estimates were staggering. The number of men whom you keep out of your factories in order that they may learn a useless drill and wear an unnecessary uniform is, to the economist, simply scandalous. Look at the result. Compare our imports and exports with yours. See the leaps and strides with which we have improved our financial position during the last ten years. We have not only recovered from the after effects of the war, but we have reached a state of prosperity which we never previously attained. You, on the other hand, are still groaning with enormous taxes. You carry a burden which is self-imposed and unnecessary. You, of all the nations, refuse to recognise the fact that the government of the great countries of the world has passed into the hands of the democracy, and that democracies will not tolerate war."

"There I join issue with you, sir," the Frenchman replied. "These are the obvious and expressed views of other European countries, yet month by month come rumours of the training of great masses of troops, far in excess of the numbers permitted by the League of Nations. There is all the time a haze of secrecy over what is going on in certain parts of Germany. And as for Russia, ostensibly the freest country in the world, Tsarism in its worst days never imposed such despotic restrictions concerning the coming and going of foreigners, in one particular district, at any rate."

"The Russian Government have certainly given us cause for complaint in that direction," Mr. Mervin Brown admitted. "Strong representations are being made to them at the present moment. On the other hand, the reason for their attitude is easily enough understood. In the days when Russia lay exhausted, foreigners took too much advantage of her, attained far too close a grip upon her great natural resources. Russia has determined that what she has left she will keep to herself. The attitude is reasonable, although I am free to admit that she is carrying her legislation against foreigners too far."

"What about the number of men she has under arms every year?" Monsieur Senn enquired.

"Russia has always a possible danger to fear from China, the new Colossus of Asia," the Prime Minister pointed out. "Even Russia herself has not made such strides within the last fifteen years as China. The secession of the Asiatic countries from the League of Nations demanded certain precautions which Russia is justified in taking."

The Frenchman had risen to his feet, but he still lingered. A tall man, of commanding presence, with olive complexion, deep brown eyes, and black hair lightly streaked with grey, Monsieur Felix Senn had been a great figure in the war of 1914–1918 and had retained since a commanding position in French politics. It had often been said that nothing but his great friendship for England had prevented his gaining the highest honours. His present mission, therefore, which was practically to end the alliance between the two countries, was a peculiarly painful one to him.

"I must tell you before we part, Mr. Mervin Brown," he said gravely, "that neither I nor many of my fellow countrymen share your optimism. You seem to have inherited the timeworn theory that the War of 1914 was entirely provoked by the junker class of Germans. That is not true. It was a people's war, and the people have never forgotten what they were pleased to consider the harsh terms of the Treaty of Peace. Then as regards Russia, have you ever considered that Russia financially and politically is more than half German? When Germany lost the war, she had one great consolation—she acquired Russia. You have compared the economic condition of France to-day with that of your country, sir. I admit your commercial supremacy, but let me tell you this. I would not, for the greatest boon the gods could offer me, see France in the same helpless state as England is in to-day."

The Prime Minister rose also to his feet. He wore an air of offended dignity.

"Monsieur Senn," he declared, "the spirit of militarism is in the blood of your country. You cannot rid yourself of it in one generation or two. But, believe me, no people's government at any time in the future, whether it be English, Russian, German, or American, will ever dare to suggest or even to dream of a war of aggression or revenge. If we are comparatively unprotected, it is because we need no protection. We hear the footfall of your marching millions, and we thank God that that sound is represented in our country by the roar of machinery and the blaze of furnaces."

The Frenchman bowed and accepted the hand which the Prime Minister offered him.

"I present to you once more, sir," he said, "the compliments and infinite regrets of Monsieur le Président."

A chapter of English history ended with the quiet passing of Monsieur Senn into the sunlit street. The latter entered his waiting automobile and drove at once to the French Embassy. The Ambassador listened in silence to his report.

"What about the Press?" was his only question.

"Monsieur le Président insists upon the truth being known," the emissary announced. "France has pledged her word against secret treaties. Besides, the honour of France must never afterwards be called in question."

The Ambassador sighed. He was new to his present post, but he had grown grey in the service of his country.

"It is the end of a one-sided arrangement," he declared. "It is incredible that these people do not realise that it is against their own country—against themselves—that this slowly fermenting hatred is being brewed. The racial enmity between Germany and France is nothing compared with the hate of antagonistic kinship between Germany and England.

However, France is the gainer by to-day's event. We have only our own frontiers to watch."

Monsieur Felix Senn wandered on to the St. Philip's Club, where he found his old friend Prince Karschoff talking in a corner of the smoking room with Nigel. They were both of them prepared for the news which he presently communicated to them. Karschoff was bitter, Nigel silent.

"Well said Carlyle that 'History is philosophy teaching by examples,'" the former expounded. "How the historian of the future will revel in this epoch! What treatises he will write, what parallels he will draw! See him point to the days when the aristocracy ruled England, and England fought and flourished; then to the epoch when the *bourgeoisie* took their place, and with a mighty effort, met a great emergency and flourished. And finally, in sympathy with the great European upheaval, in sympathy with the great natural law of change, Labour ousts both, single-eyed Labour, and down goes England, crumbling into the dust!—Let us lunch, my friends. The cuisine is still good here."

Nigel excused himself.

"I am engaged," he said. "We may meet afterwards."

"Something tells me, my dear Nigel," Karschoff declared, "that you are bent on frivolity."

"If to lunch with a woman is frivolous, I plead guilty," Nigel replied.

Karschoff's face was suddenly grave. He seemed on the point of saying something but checked himself and turned away with a little shrug of the shoulders.

"Each one to his taste," he murmured. "For my aperitif, a dash of absinthe in my cocktail; for Dorminster here, the lure of a woman's smile. Perhaps he gains. Who knows?"

XVIII

Nigel waited for his luncheon companion in the crowded vestibule of London's most famous club restaurant. He was to a certain extent out of the picture among the crowd of this new generation of pleasure seekers, on the faces of whom opulence and acquisitiveness had already laid its branding hand. The Mecca alike of musical comedy and the Stock Exchange, the place, however, still preserved a curious attraction for the foreign element in London, so that when at last Naida appeared, she was exchanging courtesies with an Italian Duchess on one side and a celebrated Russian dancer on the other. Nigel led her at once to the table which he had selected in the balcony.

"I have obeyed your wishes to the letter," he said, "and I think that you are right. Up here we are entirely alone, and, as you see, they have had the sense to place the tables a long way apart. Am I to blame, I wonder, for asking you to do so unconventional a thing as to lunch here again alone with me?"

She drew off her gloves and smiled across the table at him. Her plain, tailor-made gown, with its high collar, was the last word in elegance. The simplicity of her French hat was to prove the despair of a well-known modiste seated downstairs, who made a sketch of it on the menu and tried in vain to copy it. Even to Nigel's exacting taste she was flawless.

"Is it unconventional?" she asked carelessly. "I do not study those things. I lunch or dine with a party, generally, because it happens so. I lunch alone with you because it pleases me."

"And for this material side of our entertainment?" he enquired, smiling, as he handed her the menu card.

"A grapefruit, a quail with white grapes, and some asparagus," she replied promptly. "You see, in one respect I am an easy companion. I know exactly what I want. A mixed vermouth, if you like, yes. And now, tell me your news?"

"There is news," he announced, "which the whole world will know of before many hours are past. France has broken her pact with England."

"It is my opinion," she said deliberately, "that France has been very patient with you."

"And mine," he acknowledged. "We have now to see what will become of a fat and prosperous country with a semi-obsolete fleet and a comic opera army."

"Must we talk of serious things?" she asked softly. "I am weary of the clanking wheels of life."

He sighed.

"And yet for you," he said, "they are not grinding out the fate of your country."

"Nevertheless, I too hear them all the time," she rejoined. "And I hate them. They make one lose one's sense of proportion. After all, it is our own individual and internal life which counts. I can understand Nero fiddling while Rome burned, if he really had no power to call up fire engines."

"Are you an individualist?" he asked.

"Not fundamentally," she replied, "but I am caught up in the throes of a great reaction. I have been studying events, which it is quite true may change the destinies of the world, so intently that I have almost forgotten that, after all, the greatest thing in the world, my world, is the happiness or ill-content of Naida Karetsky. It is really of more importance to me to-day that my quail should be cooked as I like it than that England has let go her last rope."

"You are not an Englishwoman," he reminded her.

"That is of minor importance. We are all so much immersed in great affairs just now that we forget it is the small ones that count. I want my luncheon to be perfect, I want you to seem as nice to me as I have fancied you, and I want you to chase completely away the idea that you are cultivating my acquaintance for interested motives."

"That I can assure you from the bottom of my heart is not the case," he replied. "Whatever other interests I may feel in you," he added, after a moment's hesitation, "my first and foremost is a personal one."

She looked at him with gratitude in her eyes for his understanding.

"A woman in my position," she complained, "is out of place. A man ought to come over and study your deservings or your undeservings and pore over the problem of the future of Europe. I am a woman, and I am not big enough. I am too physical. I have forgotten how to enjoy myself, and I love pleasure. Now am I a revelation to you?"

"You have always been that," he told her. "You are so truthful yourself," he went on boldly, "that I shall run the risk of saying the most banal thing in the world, just because it happens to be the truth. I have felt for you since our first meeting what I have felt for no other woman in the world."

"I like that, and I am glad you said it," she declared lightly enough, although her lips quivered for a moment. "And they have put exactly the right quantity of Maraschino in my grapefruit. I feel that I am on the way to happiness. I am going to enjoy my luncheon.—Tell me about Maggie."

"I saw her yesterday," he answered. "We have arranged for her to come and live at Belgrave Square, after all."

"My terrible altruism once more," she sighed. "I had meant not to speak another serious word, and yet I must. Maggie is very clever, amazingly clever, I sometimes think, but if she had the brains of all of her sex rolled into one, she would still be facing now an impossible situation."

"Just what do you mean?" he asked cautiously.

"Maggie seems determined to measure her wits with those of Prince Shan," she said. "Believe me, that is hopeless."

She looked up at him and laughed softly.

"Oh, my dear friend," she went on, "that wooden expression is wonderful. You do not quite know where I stand, except—may I flatter myself?—as regards your personal feelings for me. Am I for Immelan and his schemes, or for your own foolish country? You do not know, so you make for yourself a face of wood."

"Where do you stand?" he asked bluntly.

"Sufficiently devoted to your interests to beg you this," she replied. "Do not let your little cousin think that she can deal with a man like Prince Shan. There can be only one end to that."

Nigel moved a little uneasily in his place.

"Prince Shan is only an ordinary human being, after all," he protested.

"That is just where you are mistaken," she declared. "Prince Shan is one of the most extraordinary human beings who ever lived. He is one of the most farseeing men in the world, and he is absolutely the most powerful."

"But China," Nigel began—

"His power extends far beyond China," she interrupted, "and there is no brain in the world to match his to-day."

"If he were a god wielding thunderbolts," Nigel observed, "he could scarcely do much harm to Maggie here in London."

"There was an artist once," she said reflectively, "who drew a caricature of Prince Shan and sent it to the principal comic paper in America. It was such a success that a little time later on he followed it up with another, which included a line of Prince Shan's ancestors. Within a month's time the artist was found murdered. Prince Shan was in China at the time."

"Are you suggesting that the artist was murdered through Prince Shan's contrivance?"

"Am I a fool?" she answered. "Do you not know that to speak disrespectfully of the ancestors of a Chinaman is unforgivable? To all appearances Prince Shan never moved from his wonderful palace in Pekin, many thousands of miles away. Yet he lifted his little finger and the man died."

"Isn't this a little melodramatic?" Nigel murmured.

"Melodrama is often nearer the truth than people think," she said. "Shall I give you another instance? I know of several."

"One more, then."

"Prince Shan was in Paris two years ago, incognito," she continued. "There was at the time a small but very fashionable restaurant in the Bois, close to the Pré Catelan. He presented himself one night there for dinner, accompanied, I believe, by La Belle Nita, the Chinese dancer who is in London to-day. As you know, there is little in Prince Shan's appearance to denote the Oriental, but for some reason or other the proprietor refused him a table. Prince Shan made no scene. He left and went elsewhere. Three nights later, the café was burnt to the ground, and the proprietor was ruined."

"Anything else?" Nigel asked.

"Only one thing more," she replied. "I have known him slightly for years. In Asia he ranks to all men as little less than a god. His palaces are filled with priceless treasures. He has the finest collection of jewels in the world. His wealth is simply inexhaustible. His appearance you appreciate. Yet I have never seen him look at a woman as he looked at your cousin the first time he met her. I was at the Ritz with my father, and I watched. I know you think that I am being foolish. I am not. I am a person with a very great deal of common sense, and I tell you that Prince Shan has never desired a thing in life to which he has not helped himself. Maggie is a clever child, but she cannot toss knives with a conjuror."

Nigel was impressed and a little worried.

"It seems absurd to think that anything could happen to Maggie here in London," he said, "after—"

He paused abruptly. Naida smiled at him.

"After her escape from Germany, I suppose you were going to say? You see, I know all about it. There was no Prince Shan in Berlin."

He shrugged his shoulders slightly.

E. PHILLIPS OPPENHEIM

"Well," he admitted, "I don't quite bring myself to believe in your terrible ogre, so I shall not worry. Tell me what news you have from Russia?"

"Political?"

"Any news."

She smiled.

"I notice," she said, "that English people are changing their attitude towards my country. A few years ago she seemed negligible to them. Now they are beginning to have—shall I call them fears? Even my kind host, I think, would like to know what is in Paul Matinsky's heart as he hears the friends of Oscar Immelan plead their cause."

"I admit it," he told her frankly. "I will go farther. I would give a great deal to know what is in your own mind to-day concerning us and our destiny. But these things are not for the moment. It was not to discuss or even to think of them that I asked you here to-day."

"Why did you invite me, then?" she asked, smiling.

"Because I wanted the pleasure of having you opposite me," he replied,—"because I wanted to know you better."

"And are you progressing?"

"Indifferently well," he acknowledged. "I seem to gain a little and slide back again. You are not an easy person to know well."

"Nothing that is worth having is easy," she answered, "and I can assure you, when my friendship is once gained, it is a rare and steadfast thing."

"And your affection?" he ventured.

Her eyes rested upon his for a moment and then suddenly drooped. A little tinge of colour stole into her cheeks. For a moment she seemed to have lost her admirable poise.

"That is not easily disturbed," she told him quietly. "I think that I must have an unfortunate temperament, there are so few people for whom I really care."

He took his courage into both hands.

"I have heard it rumoured," he said, "that Matinsky is the only man who has ever touched your heart."

She shook her head.

"That is not the truth. Paul Matinsky cares for me in his strange way, and he has a curiously exaggerated appreciation of my brain. There have been times," she went on, after a moment's hesitation, "when I myself have been disturbed by fancies concerning him, but those times have passed."

"I am glad," he said quietly.

His fingers, straying across the tablecloth, met hers. She did not withdraw them. He clasped her hand, and it remained for a moment passive in his. Then she withdrew it and leaned back in her chair.

"Is that meant to introduce a more intimate note into our conversation?" she asked, with a slight wrinkling of the forehead and the beginnings of a smile upon her lips.

"If I dared, I would answer 'yes'," he assured her.

"They tell me," she continued pensively, "that Englishmen more than any other men in the world have the flair for saying convincingly the things which they do not mean."

"In my case, that would not be true," he answered. "My trouble is that I dare not say one half of what I feel."

She looked across the table at him, and Nigel suddenly felt a great weight of depression lifted from his heart. He forgot all about his country's peril. Life and its possibilities seemed somehow all different. He was carried away by a rare wave of emotion.

"Naida!" he whispered.

"Yes?"

Her eyes were soft and expectant. Something of the gravity had gone from her face. She was like a girl, suddenly young with new thoughts.

"You know what I am going to say to you?"

"Do not say it yet, please," she begged. "Somehow it seems to me that the time has not come, though the thought of what may be in your heart is wonderful. I want to dream about it first," she went on. "I want to think."

He laughed, a strange sound almost to his own ears, for Nigel, since his uncle's death, had tasted the very depths of depression.

"I obey," he agreed. "It is well to dally with the great things. Meanwhile, they grow."

She smiled across at him.

"I hope that they may," she answered. "And you will ask me to lunch again?"

"Lunch or dine or walk or motor—whatever you will," he promised.

She reflected for a moment and then laughed. She was drawing on her gloves now, and Nigel was paying the bill.

"There are some people who will not like this," she said.

"And one," he declared, "for whom it is going to make life a Paradise."

They passed out into the street and strolled leisurely westwards. As they crossed Trafalgar Square, a stream of newsboys from the Strand were spreading in all directions. Nigel and his companion seemed suddenly surrounded by placards, all with the same headlines. They paused to read:

Triumph Of The Chancellor
Huge Reduction Of The National Debt
Total Abolition Of The Income Tax

They walked on. Naida said nothing, although she shook her head a little sorrowfully. Nigel glanced across the Square and down towards Westminster.

"They will shout themselves hoarse there this afternoon," he groaned.

For the first time she betrayed her knowledge of coming events.

"It is amazing," she whispered, "for the writing on the wall is already there."

XIX

Seated in one of the first tier boxes at the Albert Hall, in the gorgeous but obsolete uniform of a staff officer in the Russian Imperial Forces, Prince Karschoff, with Nigel on one side and Maggie on the other, gazed with keen interest at the brilliant scene below and around. The greatest city the world has ever known seemed in those days to have entered upon an orgy of extravagance unprecedented in history. Every box and every yard of dancing space on the floor beneath was crowded with men and women in wonderful fancy costumes, the women bedecked with jewels which eager merchants had brought together from every market of the world; even the men, in their silks and velvets and ruffles, carrying out the dominant note of wealth. It was a ball given for charity and under royal patronage.

"All our friends seem to be here to-night," the Prince remarked, glancing around. "I saw Naida with her father and the eternal Oscar Immelan. Chalmers is here with an exceedingly gay party, and yonder sits his Imperial Highness, looking very much the barbaric prince.—By the by," he added, glancing towards Maggie, "I thought that he was not coming?"

Maggie, who seemed a little tired, nodded quietly. It was a week or ten days later, and an early season was now in full swing.

"He told me that he was not coming," she said. "I suppose the temptation to wear that gorgeous raiment was too much for him."

"Apropos of that, there is one curious thing to be noted here with regard to clothes," the Prince continued. "Amongst the men, you find Venetian Doges, Chancellors, gallants of every age, but scarcely a single uniform. In a way, this seems typical of the passing of the militarism of your country. You are beginning to remind me of Venice in the Middle Ages. There is a new type of brain dominant here, fat instead of muscle, a citizen aristocracy instead of the lean, clear-eyed, athletic type."

Maggie moved in her place a little irritably.

"I am tired of warnings," she declared. "I wish some one could do something."

"It is impossible," the Prince pronounced solemnly. "Napoleon earned for himself a greater claim to immortality when he christened the English a nation of shopkeepers than when he won the Battle of Austerlitz. If the Englishman of to-day saw his material prosperity slipping away from him, then indeed he would be nervous and restless, ready to lean towards every wind that blew, to listen to every disquieting rumour. To-day his bank balance is prodigious, and all's well with the world.—How wonderfully Prince Shan lives up to his part to-night!"

They looked across towards the opposite box, whose single occupant, in the bright green robes of a mandarin, sat looking down upon the gay throng with an absolutely immovable expression. There was something almost regal about his air of detachment, his solitude amidst such a gay scene.

"There is one of the strangest and most consistent figures in history," Karschoff, who was in a talkative frame of mind, went on reflectively. "I honestly believe that Prince Shan considers himself to be of celestial descent, to carry in his person the honour of countless generations of Manchus. He has no intimates. Even Immelan usually has to seek an audience. What his pleasures may be, who knows?—because everything that happens with him happens behind closed walls. To-night, the door of his box is guarded as though he were more than royalty. No one is allowed to enter unless he has special permission."

"There is some one entering now," Maggie pointed out, "for the first time. Watch!"

La Belle Nita stood for a moment in the front of the box. She was dressed in the gala costume of a Chinese lady, in a cherry-coloured robe with wide sleeves, her hair, with its many jewelled ornaments, like a black pool of night, her face ghastly white with a superabundance of powder. Prince Shan turned his head slightly towards her, and though no muscle of his face moved, it was obvious that her coming was unwelcome. She began to talk. He listened with the face of a sphinx. Presently she drew back into the shadows of the box. She had thrown herself into a chair, and her face was hidden.

"La Belle Nita has made a mistake," Maggie observed. "His Serene Highness evidently had no wish to be disturbed."

Karschoff's eyes rested upon the figure in green silk, and they were filled with an unwilling admiration.

"That man is magnificent," he declared. "Watch his face now that he is speaking. Not a muscle moves, not a flash in his eyes, yet one has the fancy that he is saying terrible things."

It was obvious, a moment later, that La Belle Nita had left the box. Maggie sprang up. Her colour was a little heightened. There was a rare nervousness in her tone.

"Let us walk around and find some of the others," she suggested, turning to Nigel. "I want to dance."

They all three passed out and mingled with the dancers. Maggie put on her mask and deliberately glided into the crowd as though with the intention of losing herself. It was not until she was underneath Prince Shan's box and out of sight of its occupant that she paused. Her thoughts were in a turmoil. His presence there, after his deliberate assurance to her that he had no intention of coming, his calm and unnoticing regard of her and every one else, seemed to confirm in every way the wave of pessimism which she as well as Nigel was experiencing. She had passed Immelan in the entrance, and there was something ominously disturbing in his cool, triumphant smile. She pictured to herself the agreement signed, some nameless terror already launched. She remembered that Nigel had complained of Naida's inaccessibility during the last few days. She herself had been surprised at Prince Shan's apparent withdrawal, temporary though it might be, from the peculiar but impressive position which he had taken up with regard to her.

She stood back against the wall, in a dark corner, striving to collect her thoughts, thankful for the brief respite from conversation. A man in the costume of a monk, who had followed her across the room, touched her on the shoulder. He spoke in a quiet, unfamiliar voice with a foreign accent,

"You are Lady Maggie Trent?"

"Yes!"

"Will you please go to box number fourteen, on the second tier? There is some one there who waits for you."

"Who is it?" she asked.

The monk had glided away. Maggie, after a few minutes' reflection, slipped out into the corridor, mounted one flight of stairs, and passed along the semicircular balcony. The door of box number fourteen was ajar. She pushed it gently open and glanced in. Seated so as to be out of sight of the whole house was La Belle Nita. For a moment the two looked at each other. Then the Chinese girl sprang to her feet, made a quaint little bow, and, gliding around, closed the door behind her visitor.

"Sit down, please," she invited. "I will tell you things you may like to hear."

A sudden thought flashed into Maggie's mind. She began to see light. She obeyed at once. The two women sat well back and out of sight of the house. La Belle Nita held the handle of the door in her hand while she spoke, as though to prevent any one entering.

"I have an enemy who was once a friend," she said, "and I wish to do him evil. He is not only my enemy, but he is yours. He is the enemy of all you English people, because it is a great disaster which he plans to bring upon you."

"You speak of Prince Shan?" Maggie exclaimed.

Even at the mention of his name, the girl shook. She looked around as though fearing the shadows. She rattled the door to make sure that it was closed.

"For him whom you call Prince Shan I have worked many years, first of all in Paris, now here. I was content with small reward. That reward he now takes from me. It is my wish to betray him."

"Why do you send for me?" Maggie asked.

"Because you have been an English spy," was the quiet reply. "It may surprise you that I know that, but I do know. I have been a spy for Prince Shan in Paris. You were a spy for England in Berlin. You were a spy for your country's sake; I was a spy for love. Now I betray for hate."

"Please go on."

"Prince Shan came this time to Europe with two schemes in his mind," the girl continued. "One concerned France. That one he has discarded. Through me he learned of the military strength of France, her secret resources, of her tireless watch upon the Rhine. So he listens to Immelan, and Immelan and he together, oh, English lady, they have made a wonderful plan!"

"Are you going to tell me what it is?" Maggie asked, her eyes bright with excitement.

"I cannot tell you because I do not know," was the unwilling admission, "but I will make it so that you can discover for yourself. A few hours ago, the plan was submitted to Prince Shan. It lies in the third drawer of an ebony cabinet, in the room on the left-hand side of the hall after you have entered his house in Curzon Street."

"But no one can enter it!" Maggie exclaimed. "The place is like a fort. No stranger may pass the threshold even. The Prince has told me himself that he receives no visitors."

La Belle Nita smiled. From a pocket somewhere within the folds of her flowing gown, she produced two small keys.

"Listen," she said. "The house in Curzon Street has been called the House of Silence. There are many servants there, but they come only from beneath and when they are summoned. There is what no other person has ever possessed—the key of the front door. There is also the key of the cabinet. Prince Shan has ordered his automobile for two o'clock. It is now barely midnight."

The keys lay in the palm of Maggie's hand. Her heart had begun to beat quickly. Somehow or other, she was conscious of a thrill of excitement which she had never before experienced, even when she had sat back in her corner of the railway carriage, watching for the frontier, knowing that the wires were busy with her name, and that men who knew no mercy were on her track.

"If the servants should hear me?" she faltered.

"You say only 'I await the Prince,'" La Belle Nita murmured. "That key never leaves his own person save for one in great favour. They will believe that he gave it to you. You will be unmolested."

A queer sensation suddenly assailed Maggie. She felt extraordinarily primitive, ridiculously feminine. She looked at the girl opposite to her, the girl whose body was draped in perfumed silks, whose face was thick with rice powder, whose eyes were sad. She felt no pity. What feeling she had, she did not care to analyse.

"Is this your key?" she asked.

"It was mine once, but its use has been forbidden to me," the girl replied. "Prince Shan is a changed man. Something has come into his life of which I know nothing, but as it has come, so must I go. I give you your chance, lady, but already I weaken. Go quickly, if you go at all. Please leave me, for I am very unhappy."

Maggie stole quietly out and made her way through the jostling throng back to her own box, which for the moment was empty. She slipped on her cloak, and from the hidden spaces where she stood she looked across the auditorium. The silent figure in green silk robes was still seated in his place, his eyes following the movements of the dancers, his head a little thrown back, a slight weariness in his face. He was still alone. He still had the air of being alone because it was his desire. Once he looked up towards the box in which she was, and Maggie, although she knew she was invisible, shrank back against the wall. She set her teeth hard and looked back through the slightly misty space. An unfamiliar feeling for a moment almost choked her. She waited until she had vanquished it, then adjusted her mask and left the box.

XX

From the moment when the taxicab drove away and left her in the deserted street, Maggie was conscious of a strange sense of suppressed excitement, something more poignant and mysterious, even, than the circumstances of her adventure might account for. It was exciting enough, in its way, to play the part of a marauding thief, to find herself unexpectedly face to face with a possible solution of the great problem of Prince Shan's intentions. But beneath all this there was another feeling, more entirely metaphysical, which in a sense steadied her nerves because it filled her with a strange impression that she had lost her own identity, that she was playing somebody else's part in a novel and thrilling drama.

The street was empty when she inserted the little key in the front door. There was not a soul there to see her step in as it swung open and then softly, noiselessly, but without any conscious effort of hers, closed again behind her. She held her breath and looked around.

The hall was round, painted white and dimly lit by an overhead electric globe. In the centre was a huge green vase filled with great branches of some sort of blossoms. Not a picture hung upon the walls, nor was there any hall stand, chest, closet for coats or hats, or any of the usual furbishings of such a place. There were three rugs upon the polished floor and nothing else except a yawning stairway and closed doors. Whatever servants might be in attendance were evidently in a distant part of the building. Not a sound was to be heard. Still without any lack of courage, but oppressed with that curious sense of unreality, she turned almost automatically towards the door on the left and opened it. Again it closed behind her noiselessly. She realised that she was in one of the principal reception rooms of the house, dimly lit as the hall from a dome-shaped globe set into the ceiling. She moved a yard or two across the threshold and stood looking about her. Here again there was an almost singular absence of furniture. The walls were hung with apple-green silk, richly embroidered. There were some rugs upon the polished floor, a few quaintly carved chairs set with their backs against the wall, and opposite to her the ebony cabinet of which La Belle Nita had spoken. She moved towards it. Somehow or other, she found herself with the other key in her hand, stooping down. She counted the drawers—one, two three— fitted in the key, turned it, and realised with a little start the presence in the drawer of a roll of parchment, tied around with tape and sealed with a black seal. She laid her hand upon it, but even at that moment she felt a shiver pass through her body. There had been no sound in the room, which she could have sworn had been empty when she entered it, yet she had now a conviction that she was not alone. She turned slowly around, her lips parted, breathing quickly. Standing in the middle of the room, a grim, commanding figure in his flowing green robes, the dim light flashing upon the great diamonds in his belt, stood Prince Shan.

To Maggie at that moment came a great throbbing in her ears, a sense of remoteness from this terrible happening, followed by an intense and vital consciousness of danger. The man who had brought new things into her life, the polished gentleman of the world, with his fascinating brain and gentle courtesy, had gone. It was Prince Shan of China who stood there. She felt the chill of his contempt and disapproval in her heart. She had forfeited her high estate. She was a convicted thief,—an adventuress!

She gripped at the side of the cabinet. Her poise had gone. She had the air of a trapped animal.

"You!" she exclaimed. "How did you get here?"

He answered her without change of expression. A sense of crisis seemed to have made his tone more level, his face stony.

"It is my house," he said. "I do not often leave it. I sat in my sleeping chamber behind"—he pointed to the silken curtains through which he had passed—"I heard your entrance and guessed with pain and regret at your mission."

"But a quarter of an hour ago you were at the ball!"

"You are mistaken," he replied. "I do not attend such gatherings. I had given you my word that I should not be there."

"But I saw you," she persisted, "in that same costume!"

"Surely not," he dissented. "The person whom you saw was a gentleman from my suite, who wore the dress of an inferior mandarin. He is sometimes supposed to resemble me. I should have believed that your apprehension of such things would have informed you that no Prince of my line would wear the garments of his order for a public show."

Her fingers had left the drawer now. She stood upright, pale and desperate.

"That woman of your country, then—La Belle Nita—did she lie to me?"

　　　　　　　　　　　　　　E. PHILLIPS OPPENHEIM

"How can I tell?" he answered coldly, "because I do not know what she said."

Maggie made an effort to test her position.

"I came here as a thief," she confessed. "I am detected. What are your intentions?"

He moved very slowly a little closer to her. Maggie felt her sense of excitement grow.

"You came here as a thief," he repeated, "as a spy. Why did you not ask me for the information you desired?"

"Because you would not have told me," she replied, "at least you would not have told me the truth."

"For a price," he said, "the truth would have been yours for the asking. For a different price it is yours now."

Again without noticeable movement he seemed to have drawn nearer. The edge of that cool ebony cabinet seemed to be burning her fingers. Try however hard, she could not frame the question which had risen to her lips.

"The price," he continued, "is you—yourself. A few hours ago it was your love I craved for. Now it is yourself."

He was so near to her now that she faced the steady radiance of his wonderful eyes, so near that she could trace the faint lines about his mouth, the strong, stern immobility of his perfectly shaped, olive-tinted features.

"You are too wonderful," he went on, "to remain a daughter of the crude West. I want to take you back with me to the land where life still moves to poetry, to the land where one can live in a world unknown by these struggling hordes. You shall live in a palace where the perfume of flowers lingers always, with the sound of running water in your ears, a palace from which all sordid things and all manner of ugliness are banished because we alone have found the key to the garden of happiness."

He raised his hand, and it seemed as though unseen eyes watched them from every quarter. The silken curtains through which he had issued were drawn back by invisible hands, and the inner apartment was disclosed. Its faint illumination was obscured with purple shades. There was a high lacquer bedstead, with little ivory ladders on either side, a bedstead hung with silks of black and purple and mauve. There was a huge couch, a shrine opposite the bed, in which was a kneeling figure of black marble. A faint odour, as though from thousand-year-old sachets, very faint indeed and yet with its mead of intoxication, seemed to steal out from the room, which had borrowed from its curious hangings, its marvellous adornments, its strangely attuned atmosphere, all the mysticism of a fabled world.

"You have come," he said. "Will you stay?" The inertia seemed suddenly to leave her limbs. She threw up her head as though gasping for air, escaped, somehow or other, from the thrall of his eyes, and passed across the smooth floor with flying footsteps. Her fingers seized the handle of the door and turned it, only to find it held by some invisible fastening. She shook it passionately. There was not even sound. She turned back once more. Prince Shan had only slightly changed his position. He stood upon the threshold of the inner room, and his arms were outstretched in invitation.

"Am I a prisoner?" she sobbed.

"You came of your own free will," he replied. "You will stay for my pleasure and for the joy of my being. As for these things," he went on, moving slowly to the cabinet, picking up the pile of papers and throwing them on one side contemptuously, "these are only one's amusements. I pass my lighter hours with them. They interest me in the same manner as a chess problem. We do not care, we in the mighty East, which of you holds your head highest this side of Suez. All you western nations are to us a peck of dust outside our palace gates. Listen, dear one. We can leave, if you will, to-night, and top the clouds before sunrise. And I promise you this," he went on, "when you pass from the greyness of these sordid lands into the everlasting sunshine of the East, you will not care any longer about these people who go about the world on all fours. Day by day you will know what life and love mean. You will find the cloying weight of material things pass from your brain and body, and the joy of holy and wonderful living take their place."

Her whole being was in a turmoil. She drew nearer to the papers upon the table. She was now within a yard of Prince Shan himself. He made no effort to intercept her, no movement of any sort to stop her. Only his eyes never left her face, and she felt a madness which seemed to be choking the life out of her, a pounding of her heart against her ribs, a strange and wonderful joy, a joy in which there was no fear, a joy of new things and new hopes. With the papers for which she had come only a few yards away, she forgot them. She turned her head slowly. His arms seemed to steal out from those long, silken sleeves. She suddenly felt herself held in a wonderful embrace.

E. PHILLIPS OPPENHEIM

"Dear lady of all my desires," he whispered in her ear, "you shall make me happy and find the secret of happiness yourself in giving, in suffering, in love."

For a long and wonderful moment she lay in his arms. She felt the soft burning of his kisses, the call of the room with its intoxicating, yet strangely ascetic perfume, the room to which all the time he seemed to be gently leading her. And then a flood of strange, alien recollections and realisations seemed to bring her from a better place back to a worse,—the sound of a passing taxicab, the distant booming of Big Ben, sounds of the world outside, the actual day-by-day world, with its day-by-day code of morals, the world in which she lived, and her friends, and all that had made life for her. She drew away, and he watched the change in her.

"I want to go!" she cried. "Let me go!"

"You are no prisoner," he assured her sadly.

He clapped his hands. She had reached the door by now and found the handle yield to her fingers. Outside in the hall, the front door stood open, and a heavy rain was beating in on the white flags. She looked around. She was in her own atmosphere here. Their eyes met, and his were very sorrowful.

"My servants are assembling," he said. "You will find a car at your service."

Even then she hesitated. There was a strange return of the wonderful emotion of a few minutes ago. She hoped almost painfully that he would call. Instead, he lifted the silk hangings and passed out of sight. Somehow or other, she made her way down the hall. A butler stood upon the steps, another servant was holding open the door of a limousine just drawn up. She had no distinct recollection of giving any address. She simply threw herself back amongst the cushions. It was not until they were in Piccadilly that she suddenly remembered that she had left upon the table the papers he had scornfully offered her. Then she began to laugh.

XXI

I t chanced that the box was empty when Maggie, with flying footsteps, hastened down the corridor and pushed open the door. She sank into a chair, her knees trembling, her senses still dazed. Deliberately, although with hot and trembling fingers, she folded over and tore into small pieces a programme of the dances, which she had picked up from an adjoining chair. The action, insignificant though it was, seemed to bring her back into touch with the real and actual world, the world of music and wild gayety, of swiftly moving feet, of laughter and languorous voices. For a brief space of time she had escaped, she had wandered a little way into an unknown country, a country from whose thrilling dangers she had emerged with a curious feeling that life would never be altogether the same again. She glanced at the clock at the back of the box. She had been absent from the Hall altogether only about an hour and twenty minutes. There was still at least an hour before it would be possible for her to plead weariness and escape. And opposite, in the shadows of the distant box, the mock Prince Shan seemed always to be gazing at her with that cryptic smile upon his lips.

Presently the door was stealthily opened. A face as pale as death, with black eyes like pieces of coal, was framed for a moment in the shadowed slit. A little waft of familiar perfume stole in. La Belle Nita, her flaming lips widely parted, as soon as she recognised the sole occupant of the box, crept through the opening and closed the door again.

"You are here?" she exclaimed incredulously. "Your courage failed you? You did not go?"

"I have been and returned," Maggie answered. "Now tell me what I have done that you should have plotted this thing against me?"

The girl sat on the edge of a chair and for a moment hummed the refrain of a sad chant, as she rocked slowly backwards and forwards.

"'What have you done?' the rose asked the butterfly. 'What have you done?' the mimosa blossom asked the little blue bird, whose wings fluttered amongst her leaves. 'You have taken love from me, love which is the blossom of life.'"

"It sounds very picturesque," Maggie said coldly, "but I do not follow your allegory. What I want to know is why you lied to me, why you sent me to that house to meet Prince Shan?"

"How did I lie to you?" Nita demanded. "The papers you sought were there. Were they not yours for the asking, or was the price too great?"

"The papers were there, certainly," Maggie acquiesced, "but you knew very well—"

She stopped short. Slowly the Oriental idea of it all was beginning to frame itself in her mind. She dimly understood the bewilderment in the other's face.

"The papers were there, and he, the most wonderful of all men, was there," Nita murmured, "yet you leave him while the night is yet young, you return here without them!"

Maggie rose from her chair, moved to the side table and poured herself out a glass of wine, which she drank hastily. Anything to escape from the scornful wonder of those questioning eyes!

"I did not go there," she said, "to make bargains with Prince Shan. I believed as you wished me to believe, that he was here in that box. I believed that I should have found the house empty, should have found what I wanted and have escaped with it. Why did you do this thing? Why did you send me on that errand when you knew that Prince Shan was there?"

"It was my desire that he should know that you are no different from other women," was the calm reply. "I was a spy for him. You are a spy—against him."

"It was a deliberate plot, then!" Maggie exclaimed, trying to feel the anger which she imparted to her tone.

La Belle Nita suddenly laughed, softly and like a bird.

"You very, very foolish Englishwoman," she said. "A hand leaned down from Heaven, and you liked better to stay where you were, but I am glad."

"And why?"

"Because I have been his slave," the girl continued. "At odd, strange moments he has shown me a little love, he has let me creep into a small corner of his heart. Now I am cast out, and there is no more life for me because there is no more love, and there is no more love because, having felt his, no other can come after. Here have I sat with all the tortures of Hell burning in my blood because I knew that you and he were there alone, because I was never sure that, after all, I was not doing my lord's will. And now I know that I suffered in vain. You did not understand."

Maggie looked across at her visitor reflectively. She was beginning to regain her poise.

"Listen," she said, "did you seriously expect me to accept Prince Shan as a lover?"

The girl's eyes were round with wonder.

"It would be your great good fortune," she murmured, "if he should offer you so wonderful a thing."

Maggie laughed,—persisted in her laugh, although it sounded a little hard and the mirth a little forced.

"I cannot reason with you," she declared, "because you would not understand. If you love him so much, why not go back to him? You will find him quite alone. I dare say you know the secrets of his lockless doors and hordes of unseen servants."

La Belle Nita rose to her feet. About her lips there flickered the faintest smile.

"Young English lady," she said, "I shall not go, because I am shut for ever out of his heart. But listen; would you have me go?"

For a moment Maggie's poise was gone again. A strange uncertainty was once more upon her. She was terrified at her own feelings. The smile on the other's lips deepened and then passed away.

"Ah," she murmured, as with a little bow she turned towards the door, "you are not all snow and ice, then! There is something of the woman in you. He must have known that. I am better content."

Alone in the box, Maggie was confronted once more with spectres. She felt all the fear and the sweetness of this new awakening. The old dangers and problems, the danger of life and death, the problem of her well-ordered days, fell away from her as trifles. There was wilder music in the world than any to which she had yet listened,—music which seemed to be awakening vibrant melodies in her terrified heart. The curtain which hung about the forbidden world had been suddenly lifted. Little shivers of fear convulsed her. Her standards were confused, her whole sense of values disturbed. Her primal virginity, left to itself because it had never needed a guard, had suddenly become a questioning thing. She sat there face to face with this new phase in her life. She was not even conscious of the abrupt pause in the music, the agitated murmur of voices, the sudden cessation of that rhythmical sweep of footsteps on the floor below.

The door of the box was once more opened. Naida, attired as a lady of the Russian Court, entered, followed by Nigel. Both were obviously disturbed. Nigel, who was in ordinary evening dress, carrying his discarded mask in his hand, was paler than usual and exceedingly grave.

Naida's dark eyes, too, seemed filled with a sense of awesome things. Almost at the same moment, Maggie realised for the first time that the music had ceased, that there was a hush outside, curiously perceptible, almost audible.

"What has happened?" she asked breathlessly.

Nigel had poured out a glass of wine and was holding it to Naida's lips.

"Something very terrible," he said quietly. "Prince Shan was murdered in his box there a few minutes ago."

Maggie half rose to her feet. The walls seemed spinning round. Then she looked across the great empty space. The still figure in the apple-green coat had disappeared.

"Prince Shan was murdered in that box," she repeated, "a few minutes ago?"

"Yes!" Nigel assented gravely. "He seems to have feared something of the sort, for he had two servants on guard outside and announced that he was not receiving visitors to-night. No one knows any particulars, but a number of people in the auditorium saw him fall sideways from his chair. When he was picked up, there was a small dagger through his heart."

"Through Prince Shan's heart?" Maggie persisted wildly.

"Yes!"

Suddenly she began to laugh. It was a strange, hysterical ebullition of feeling, frankly horrifying. Naida gazed at her with distended eyes.

"Prince Shan has never been here!" Maggie explained brokenly. "He has never left his house in Curzon Street! He is there now!"

Nigel shook his head.

"What is the matter with you, Maggie?" he demanded. "Every one has seen Prince Shan here. You spoke of him yourself. He was in the box exactly opposite."

She shook her head.

"That was one of his suite," she cried. "I know! I tell you I know!" she went on, her voice rising a little. "Prince Shan is safe in his house in Curzon Street."

"How can you possibly know this, Maggie?" Naida intervened eagerly.

"Because I left him there half an hour ago," was the tremulous reply.

XXII

There is in the Anglo-Saxon temperament an almost feverish desire to break away from any condition of strain, a sort of shamefaced impulse to discard emotionalism. The strange hush which had lent a queer sensation of unreality to all that was passing in the great building was without any warning brought to an end. Whispers swelled into speech, and speech into almost a roar of voices. Then the music struck up, although at first there were few who cared to dance. There were many who, like Maggie and her companions, silently left their places and hurried homewards.

In the limousine scarcely a word was spoken. Maggie leaned back in her seat, her face dazed and expressionless. Opposite to her, Nigel sat with set, grim face, looking with fixed stare out of the window at the deserted streets. Of the three, Naida seemed more on the point of giving way to emotion. They had passed Hyde Park Corner, however, before a word was spoken. Then it was she who broke the silence.

"Where do we go to first?" she demanded.

"To the Milan Court," Nigel replied.

"You are taking me home first, then?"

"Yes!"

She was silent for a moment. Then she leaned forward and touched the window.

"Pull that down, please," she directed. "I am stifling."

He obeyed, and the rush of cold, wet air had a curiously quietening effect upon the nerves of all of them. Raindrops hung from the leaves of the lime trees and still glittered upon the windowpane. On the way towards the river, the masses of cloud were tinged with purple, and faintly burning stars shone out of unexpectedly clear patches of sky. The night of storm was over, but the wind, dying away before the dawn, seemed to bring with it all the sweetness of the cleansed places, to be redolent even of the budding trees and shrubs,—the lilac bushes, drooping with their weight of moisture, and the pink and white chestnut blossoms, dashed to pieces by the rain but yielding up their lives with sweetness. The streets, in that single hour between the hurrying homewards of the belated reveller and the stolid tramp of the early worker, were curiously empty and seemed to gain in their loneliness a new dignity. Trafalgar

Square, with the National Gallery in the background, became almost classical; Whitehall the passageway for heroes.

"What does it all mean?" Naida asked, almost pathetically.

It was Maggie who answered. Her tone was lifeless, but her manner almost composed.

"It means that the attempt to assassinate Prince Shan has failed," she said. "Prince Shan told me himself that he had no intention of going to the ball. He kept his word. The man who was murdered was one of his suite."

"But how do you know this?" Naida persisted.

"You heard what I told you in the box," was the quiet reply. "I shall explain—as much as I can explain—to Nigel when we get home. He can tell you everything later on to-day at lunch-time, if you like."

"It has been one of the strangest nights I ever remember," Naida declared, after a brief pause. "Oscar Immelan, who was dining with us, arrived half an hour late. I have never seen him in such a condition before. He had the air of a broken man."

"Have you any idea of what had happened?" Nigel asked.

"Only this," Naida replied. "We saw Prince Shan last night. He spent several hours with us. I may be wrong, but I came to the conclusion then that he had at any rate modified his views about the whole situation since his arrival in England."

Again there was a brief silence. The minds of all three of them were busy with the same thought. Prince Shan's word had been spoken and Immelan's hopes dashed to the ground,—and within a few hours, this murder! They nursed the thought, but no one put it into words.

A sleepy-eyed porter opened the door of the car outside the Milan Court. Naida gathered herself together with a little shiver.

"I think that after to-night," she said quietly, "there need be no secrets between any of us."

Nigel held her hand in his. Their eyes met, and both of them were conscious, in that moment, of closer personal relations, of the passing of a certain sense of strain. She even smiled as she turned away.

"To-morrow," she concluded, "there must be a great exchange of confidences. I am lunching at Belgrave Square, if Maggie has not forgotten, and I shall tell you then what I have written to Paul Matinsky. I showed it to Prince Shan yesterday. Good night!"

She patted Maggie's hand affectionately and flitted away. The revolving doors closed behind her, and the car swung out once more into the Strand, glided down the Mall, past Buckingham Palace, and stopped at last before the great, lifeless house in Belgrave Square. Nigel opened the front door with a latchkey and turned on the light.

"You won't mind sparing me a few minutes?" he begged.

"I suppose not," she answered, shivering.

He led the way to the study. She threw off her cloak and sank into the depths of one of the big easy-chairs. She looked very frail and rather pathetic as she leaned her head against the chair back. Now that the excitement was over, the strain of the emotion she had experienced showed in the violet shadows under her eyes and in the droop of her shoulders.

"I am tired," she said plaintively.

Nigel came over and sat on the arm of her chair.

"Tell me what happened to-night, Maggie."

"The little Chinese girl sent for me to go to her box," she explained. "She told me where in Prince Shan's house were hidden the papers which revealed the understanding between Immelan and himself. She gave me a key of the house and a key of the cabinet. We could both see the man whom I believed to be Prince Shan seated in his box. She assured me that he would be there for the next two hours. I went to the house in Curzon Street."

"Well?"

His monosyllable was sharp and incisive. His face was grey and anxious. She herself remained lifeless. All that there was of emotion between them seemed to have become vested in his searching eyes.

"I found what I believe to have been the papers. They were in the cabinet, just where she had told me. Then I turned around and found Prince Shan watching me. He had been there all the time."

"Go on, please."

"At first he said little, but I knew that he was very angry. I have never felt so ashamed in my life."

"You must tell me the rest, please."

She stirred uneasily in her chair.

"It is very difficult," she confessed frankly.

"Remember," he persisted, "that in a way, Maggie, I am your guardian. I am responsible, too, for anything which may happen to you whilst you are engaged in work for the good of our cause. You seem to have walked into a trap. Did he threaten you, or what?"

"There was nothing definite," she answered, "and yet—he made me understand."

"Made you understand what?"

"His wishes," she replied, looking up coolly. "He offered me the papers."

"That damned Chinaman!"

There was a cold light in her eyes which Nigel had met with before and dreaded.

"You forget yourself, Nigel," she said. "Prince Shan is a great nobleman."

"The rest? Tell me the rest," he demanded.

"I am here," she reminded him.

"And the papers?"

"I came away without them."

He turned, and, walking to the window, threw it open. The dawn had become almost silvery, and the leaves of the overhanging trees were rustling in the faintest of breezes. Presently he came back.

"What exactly are your feelings for this man, Maggie?" he asked.

For the first time he was struck with a certain pathos in her immobile face. She looked up at him, and there was a gleam almost of fear in her eyes.

"I don't know, Nigel," she confessed.

He moved restlessly about the room, seemed to notice for the first time the whisky and soda set out upon the sideboard and the open box of cigarettes. He helped himself and came back.

"Did you read the papers?" he asked.

She shook her head.

"I had no chance."

"You don't know for certain what they were about?"

"I think I do," she replied. "I believe they contained the text of the agreement between Immelan and Prince Shan. I believe they would have shown us exactly what we have to fear."

He stood there for a moment thoughtfully.

"To-night," he said, "I find it difficult to concentrate upon these things. Naida was extraordinarily hopeful. She has seen Prince Shan, and between them I believe that they have decided to let Oscar Immelan's scheme alone. Karschoff, too, has heard rumours. He is of the same opinion. Somehow or other, though, I seem to have lost my sense of perspective. A greater fear has come into my heart, Maggie."

She rose to her feet and laid her hands upon his shoulders.

"Nigel," she whispered, "I cannot answer you. I cannot say what you would like me to say, although, on the other hand, there is no surety of what you seem to fear. I am going to bed. I am very tired."

A feeble shaft of sunlight stole into the room, flickered and passed away, then suddenly reappeared. Nigel turned and opened the door, and she passed out, curiously silent and absorbed. He looked after her, perplexed and worried. Suddenly a strangely commonplace, yet—in the silence of the house and the great hall—an almost dramatic sound startled him. The front doorbell rang sharply. After a moment's hesitation, he hurried to it himself. Karschoff stood upon the steps, still in his evening clothes, his face a little drawn and haggard in the bright light.

"I could not resist coming in, Nigel," he said. "I saw the light in the study from outside. Is there any definite news?"

Nigel drew him inside.

"There are indications," he replied cautiously, "that the present danger is passing."

Karschoff nodded.

"I gathered so from Naida," he admitted. "Prince Shan, though, is the pivot upon which the whole thing turns. You have heard nothing final from him?"

"Nothing! Tell me, was any one arrested at the Albert Hall?"

"No one. The murdered man, as I suppose you have heard, was Sen Lu, one of the Prince's secretaries."

"The whole thing seems strange," Nigel remarked. "Do you suppose Prince Shan knew that an attempt upon his life was likely to-night?"

Karschoff shook his head doubtfully.

"It is difficult to say. These Orientals contrive to surround themselves with such an atmosphere of mystery. But from what I know of Prince Shan," he went on, "I do not think that he is one to shirk danger—even from the assassin's dagger."

A milk cart drew up with a clatter outside. There was the sound of the area gate being opened. Karschoff put on his hat. He looked Nigel in the face.

"Maggie," he began—

Nigel nodded understandingly as he threw open the front door.

"I'll tell you about it to-morrow," he promised, "or rather later on to-day. She's a little overwrought. Otherwise—there's nothing."

Karschoff turned away with a sigh of relief.

"I am glad," he said. "Prince Shan is the soul of honour according to his own standard, but these Orientals—one never knows. I am glad, Nigel."

XXIII

In his spacious reception room, with its blue walls, the high vases of flowers, the faint odour of incense, its indefinable ascetic charm, Prince Shan sat in his high-backed chair whilst Li Wen, his trusted secretary talked. Li Wen was very eloquent. His tone was never raised, he never forgot that he was speaking to a being of a superior world. He had a great deal to say, however, and he was eager to say it. Prince Shan, as he listened, smoked a long cigarette in a yellow tube. He wore a ring in which was set an uncut green stone on the fourth finger of his left hand. Although the hour was barely nine o'clock, he was shaved and dressed as though for a visit of ceremony. He listened to Li Wen gravely and critically.

"I am sorry about the little one," he said, looking through the cloud of tobacco smoke up towards the ceiling. "Nita has been very useful. She has been as faithful, too, as is possible for a woman."

Li Wen bowed and waited. He knew better than to interrupt.

"It was through the information which Nita brought me," his master went on, "that I have been able to check the truth of Immelan's statement as to the French dispositions and the *rapprochement* with Italy. Nita has served me very well indeed. What she has done in this matter, she has done in a moment of caprice."

"My lord," Li Wen ventured, "a woman is of no account in the plans of the greatest. She is like a leaf blown hither or thither on the winds of love or jealousy. She may be used, but she must be discarded."

"It is a strange world, this western world," Prince Shan mused. "In our own country, Li Wen, we plot or we fight, we build the great places, climb to the lofty heights, and when we rest we pluck flowers, and women are our flowers. But here, while one builds, the women are there; while one climbs, the women are in the way. They jostle the thoughts, they disturb the emotions, not only of the poet and the pleasure seeker, but of the man who hews his way upwards to the goal he seeks. And it is very deliberate, Li Wen. An Englishman eats and drinks in public and places opposite him a flower he has plucked or hopes to pluck. He drugs himself deliberately. Half the time when he should be soaring in his thoughts, he descends of deliberate intent. Instead of his flower, he makes his woman the partner of his grossness."

"The master speaks," Li Wen murmured. "But what of the woman? She awaits your pleasure."

"I shall hear what she has to say," Prince Shan decided.

Walking backwards as nimbly as a cat, his head drooped, his hands in front of him, Li Wen left his master's presence. A moment later he reappeared, ushering in La Belle Nita. Prince Shan waved him away. The girl came slowly forward, pale and trembling, smouldering fires in her narrow eyes. Not a muscle of Prince Shan's face moved. He watched her approach in silence. She sank on to the floor by the side of his chair.

"What is my master's will?" she asked.

Prince Shan looked downwards at her, and she began to tremble again. There was nothing threatening in his eyes, nothing menacing in his expression. Nevertheless, she felt the chill of death.

"You have done me many good and faithful services, Nita," he said. "What evil spirit has put it into your brain that it would be a good thing to deceive me?"

Her scarlet lips opened and closed again.

"How have I deceived?" she faltered. "I gave the keys to the woman with the blue eyes, and I sent her to my lord. It was a hard thing to do that, but I did it. Was there any risk of evil? My lord was here to deal with her."

"Why did you do this thing, Nita?" he asked.

"My lord knows," she answered simply. "I did it to bring evil upon this English woman whom he has preferred. I did it that he might understand. It was my lord himself who told me that she was a spy. Now it is proved."

Prince Shan's fingers stole into the pocket of his coat. He held out a crumpled sheet of paper, on which was written a single sentence. The girl began to shiver.

"You have been very anxious indeed, Nita," he said, "to bring evil upon this woman. This is the message you sent to Immelan. Do you recognise your words? Listen, these are your words:

"'The greatest of all will desert you, if the Englishwoman whom he loves is not speedily removed. Even to-night he may give papers into her hand, and your secret will be known.'"

The girl sat transfixed. She seemed to have lost all power of speech.

"That is a copy of the message which you sent to Immelan," he told her sternly.

"It is the terrible Li Wen," she faltered. "He has the second sight. The devil walks with him."

"The devil is sometimes a useful confederate," her companion continued equably. "You warned Immelan that it was in my mind to refuse his terms and to open my heart to the Englishwoman, and you seduced Sen Lu to carry your message. Yet your judgment was at fault. The hand of Immelan was stretched out against me, and me alone. But for my knowledge of these things, I might have sat in the place of Sen Lu, who rightly died in my stead. What have you to say?"

She rose to her feet. He made no movement, but his eyes watched her, and the muscles of his body stiffened. He watched the white hand which stole irresolutely towards the loose folds of her coat.

"You ask me why I have done this," she cried, "but you already know. It is because you have taken this woman with the blue eyes into your heart."

"If that were true," he answered, "of what concern is it to others? I am Prince Shan."

"You sent me here to breathe this cursed western atmosphere," she moaned, "to drink in their thoughts and see with their eyes. I see and know the folly of it all, but who can escape? Jealousy with us is a disease. Over there one creeps away like a hurt animal because there is nothing else. Here it is different. The Frenchwoman, the Englishwoman, who loses her lover—she does not fold her hands. She strikes, she is a wronged creature. I too have felt that."

Her master sat for long in silence.

"You are right," he pronounced. "I shall try to be just. You are a person of small understanding. You have never made any effort to live with your head in the clouds. Let that be so. The fault was mine."

"I do not wish to live," she cried.

He shrugged his shoulders.

"Live or die—what does it matter?" he answered indifferently. "With life there is pain, and with death there is none, but if you choose life, remember this. The woman with the blue eyes, as you call her, has become the star of my life. If harm should come to her, not only you, but every one of your family and race, in whatsoever part of the world they may be, will leave this life in agony."

The girl stood and wondered.

"My lord thinks so much of a plaything?" she murmured.

Prince Shan frowned. His finely shaped, silky eyebrows almost met. She covered her eyes and drooped her head.

"We of the East," he said, "although we are the mightier race, progress slowly, because the love of new things is not with us. Something of western ways I have learned, and the love of woman. It is not for a plaything I desire her whom we will not name. She shall sit by my side and rule. I shall wed her with my brain as with my body. Our minds will move together. We shall feel the same shivering pleasure when we rule the world with great thoughts as when our bodies touch. I shall teach her to know her soul, even as my own has been revealed to me."

"No woman is worthy of this, my lord," the girl faltered.

He waved his hand and she stole away. At the door he stopped her.

"Do you go to life or death, Nita?" he asked.

She looked at him with a great sorrow.

"I am a worthless thing," she replied. "I go where my lord's words have sent me."

Li Wen reappeared presently for an appointed audience. He brought messages.

"Highness," he announced, "there is a code dispatch here from Ki-Chou. An American gained entrance to the City last week. Yesterday he left by æroplane for India. He was overtaken and captured. It is feared, however, that he has agents over the frontier, for no papers were found upon him."

"It was a great achievement," Prince Shan said thoughtfully. "No other foreigner has ever passed into our secret city. Is there word as to how he got there?"

"He came as a Russian artificer from that city in Russia of which we do not speak," Li Wen replied. "He brought letters, and his knowledge was great."

"His name?" the Prince asked.

"Gilbert Jesson, Highness. His passport and papers refer to Washington, but his message, if he sent one, is believed to have come to London."

"The man must die," the Prince said calmly. "That, without doubt, he expects. Yet the news is not serious. My heart has spoken for peace, Li Wen."

Li Wen bowed low. His master watched him curiously.

"If I had asked it, Li Wen, where would your counsel have led?"

"Towards peace, Highness. I do not trust Immelan. It is not in such a manner that China's Empire shall spread. There are ancestors of mine who would turn in their graves to find China in league with a western Power."

"You are a wise man, Li Wen," his master declared. "We hold the mastery of the world. What shall we do with it?"

"The mightiest sword is that which enforces peace," was the calm reply. "Highness, the lady whom you were expecting waits in the anteroom."

Prince Shan nodded. He welcomed Naida, who was ushered in a moment or two later, with rather more than his usual grave and pleasant courtesy, leading her himself to a chair.

"I wondered," she confessed, "if I were ever to be allowed to see inside your wonderful house."

"It is my misfortune to be compelled to pay so brief a visit to this country," he replied. "As a rule, it gives me great pleasure to open my rooms three evenings and entertain those who care to come and see me."

"I have heard of your entertainments," she said, smiling. "Prima donnas sing. You rob the capitals of Europe to find your music. Then the great Monsieur Auguste is lured from Paris to prepare your supper, and not a lady leaves without some priceless jewel."

"I entertain so seldom," he reminded her. "I fear that the fame of my feasts has been exaggerated."

"When do you leave, Prince?" she asked him.

"Within a few days," he replied.

"I come for your last word," she announced. "All that I have written to Paul Matinsky you know."

"The last word is not yet to be spoken," he said. "This, however, you may tell Matinsky. The scheme of Oscar Immelan has been laid before me. I have rejected it."

"In what other way, then, would you use your power?" she asked.

He made no answer. She watched him with a great and growing curiosity.

"Prince," she said, "they tell me that you are a great student of history."

"I have read what is known of the history of most of the countries of the world," he admitted.

"There have been men," she persisted, "who have dealt in empires for the price of a woman's smile."

"Such men have loved," he said, "as I love."

"Yet for you life has always been a great and lofty thing," she reminded him. "You could not stand where you do if you had not realised the beauty and wonder of sacrifice. Fate has given the peace of the world into your keeping. You will not juggle with the trust?"

He rose to his feet. A servant stood almost immediately at the open door.

"Fate and an American engineer," he remarked with a smile. "I thank you, dear lady, for your visit. You will hear my news before I leave."

She looked into his eyes for a moment.

"It is a great decision," she said, "which rests with you!"

XXIV

An hour or so later, Prince Shan left his house in Curzon Street and, followed at a discreet distance by two members of his household, strolled into the Park. It had pleased him that morning to conform rigorously to the mode of dress adopted by the fashionable citizens of the country which he was visiting. Few people, without the closest observation, would have taken him for anything but a well-turned-out, exceedingly handsome and distinguished-looking Englishman. He carried himself with a faint air of aloofness, as though he moved amongst scenes in which he had no actual concern, as though he were living, in thought at any rate, in some other world. The morning was brilliantly sunny, and both the promenade and the Row were crowded. Slightly hidden behind a tree, he stood and watched. A gay crowd of promenaders passed along the broad path, and the air was filled with the echo of laughter, the jargon of the day, intimate references to a common world, invitations lightly given and lightly accepted. It was Sunday morning, in a season when colour was the craze of the moment, and the women who swept by seemed to his rather mystical fancy like the flowers in some of the great open spaces he knew so well, stirred into movement by a soft wind. They were very beautiful, these western women; handsome, too, the men with whom they talked and flirted. Always they had that air, however, of absolute complacency, as though they felt nothing of the quest which lay like a thread of torture amongst the nerves of Prince Shan's being. There was no more distinguished figure among the men there than he himself, and yet the sense of alienation grew in his heart as he watched. There were many familiar faces, many to whom he could have spoken, no one who would not have greeted him with interest, even with gratification. And yet he had never been so deeply conscious of the gulf which lay between the oriental fatalism of his life and ways and the placid self-assurance of these westerners, so well-content with the earth upon which their feet fell. He had judged with perfect accuracy the place which he held in their thoughts and estimation. He was something of a curiosity, his title half a joke, the splendour of his long race a thing unrealisable by these scions of a more recent aristocracy. Yet supposing that this new wonder had not come into his life, that Immelan had been a shade more eloquent, had pleaded his cause upon a higher level, that

Naida Karetsky also had formed a different impression of the world which he was studying so earnestly,—what a transformation he could have brought upon this light-hearted and joyous scene! The scales had so nearly balanced; at the bottom of his heart he was conscious of a certain faint contempt for the almost bovine self-satisfaction of a nation without eyes. Literature and painting, art in all its far-flung branches, even science, were suffering in these days from a general and paralysing inertia. Life which demanded no sacrifice of anybody was destructive of everything in the nature of aspiration. Sport seemed to be the only incentive to sobriety, the desire to live long in this fat land the only brake upon an era of self-indulgence. He looked eastwards to where his own millions were toiling, with his day-by-day maxims in their ears, and it seemed to his elastic fancy that he was inhaling a long breath of cooler and more vigorous life.

The current of his reflections was broken. He had moved a little towards the rails, and he was instantly aware of the girl cantering towards him,—a slight, frail figure, she seemed, upon a great bay horse. She wore a simple brown habit and bowler hat, and she sat her horse with that complete lack of self-consciousness which is the heritage of a born horsewoman. She was looking up at the sky as she cantered towards him, with no thought of the crowds passing along the promenade. Yet, as she drew nearer, she suddenly glanced down, and their eyes met. As though obeying his unspoken wish, she reined in her horse and came close to the rails behind which he stood for a moment bareheaded. There was the faintest smile upon her lips. She was amazingly composed. She had asked herself repeatedly, almost in terror, how they should meet when the time came. Now that it had happened, it seemed the most natural thing in the world. She was scarcely conscious even of embarrassment.

"You are demonstrating to the world," she remarked, "that the reports of your death this morning were exaggerated?"

"I had forgotten the incident," he assured her calmly.

His callousness was so unaffected that she shivered a little.

"Yet this Sen Lu, this man for whom you were mistaken, was an intimate member of your household, was he not?"

"Sen Lu was a very good friend," Prince Shan answered. "He did his duty for many years. If he knows now that his life was taken for mine, he is happy to have made such atonement."

She manoeuvred her horse a little to be nearer to him.

"Why was Sen Lu murdered?" she asked.

"There are those," he replied, "of whom I myself shall ask that question before the day is over."

"You have an idea, then?" she persisted.

"If," he said, "you desire my whole confidence, it is yours."

She sat looking between her horse's ears.

"To tell you the truth," she confessed, "I do not know what I desire. Your philosophy, I suppose, does not tolerate moods. I shall escape from them some time, I expect, but just now I seem to have found my way into a maze. The faces of these people don't even seem real to me, and as for you, I am perfectly certain that you have never been in China in your life."

"Tell me the stimulant that is needed to raise you from your apathy," he asked. "Will you find it in the rapid motion of your horse—a very noble animal—in the joy of this morning's sunshine and breeze, or in the toyland where these puppets move and walk?" he added, glancing down the promenade. "Dear Lady Maggie, I beg permission to pay you a visit of ceremony. Will you receive me this afternoon?"

She knew then what it was that she had been hoping for. She looked down at him and smiled.

"At four o'clock," she invited.

She nodded, touched her horse lightly with the whip, and cantered off. Prince Shan found himself suddenly accosted by a dozen acquaintances, all plying him with questions. He listened to them with an amused smile.

"The whole affair is a very simple one," he said. "A member of my household was assassinated last night. It was probably a plot against my own life. Those things are more common with us, perhaps, than over here."

"Jolly country, China, I should think," one of the younger members of the group remarked. "You can buy a man's conscience there for ninepence."

Prince Shan looked across at the speaker gravely.

"The market value here," he observed, "seems a little higher, but the supply greater."

"*Touché!*" Karschoff laughed. "There is another point of view, too. The further east you go, the less value life has. Westwards, it becomes an absolute craze to preserve and coddle it, to drag it out to its furthermost span. The American millionaire, for example, has a resident physician attached to his household and is likely to spend the aftermath of his life in a semi-drugged and comatose condition. And in the East, who cares? If not to-day—to-morrow! Inevitability, which is the nightmare of the West, is the philosophy of the East. By the by, Prince," he added, "have you any theory as to last night's attempt?"

"That is just the question," Prince Shan replied, "which two very intelligent gentlemen from Scotland Yard asked me this morning. Theory? Why should I have a theory?"

"The attempt was without a doubt directed against you," Karschoff observed. "Do you imagine that it was personal or political?"

"How can I tell?" the Prince rejoined carelessly. "Why should any one desire my death? These things are riddles. Ah! Here comes my friend Immelan!" he went on. "Immelan, help us in this discussion. You are not one of those who place the gift of life above all other things in the world!"

"My own or another's?" Immelan asked, with blunt cynicism.

"I trust," was the bland reply, "that you are, as I have always esteemed you, an altruist."

"And why?"

Prince Shan shrugged his shoulders. He was a very agreeable figure in the centre of the little group of men, the hands which held his malacca cane behind his back, the smile which parted his lips benign yet cryptic.

"Because," he explained, "it is a great thing to have more regard for the lives of others than for one's own, and there are times," he added, "when it is certainly one's own life which is in the more precarious state."

There was a little dispersal of the crowd, a chorus of congratulations and farewells. Immelan and Prince Shan were left alone. The former seemed to have turned paler. The sun was warm, and yet he shivered.

"Just what do you mean by that, Prince?" he asked.

"You shall walk with me to my house, and I will tell you," was the quiet reply.

XXV

I suppose," Immelan suggested, as the two men reached the house in Curzon Street, "it would be useless to ask you to break your custom and lunch with me at the Ritz or at the club?"

His companion smiled deprecatingly.

"I have adopted so many of your western customs," he said apologetically. "To this lunching or dining in public, however, I shall never accustom myself."

Immelan laughed good-naturedly. The conversation of the two men on their way from the Park had been without significance, and some part of his earlier nervousness seemed to be leaving him.

"We all have our foibles," he admitted. "One of mine is to have a pretty woman opposite me when I lunch or dine, music somewhere in the distance, a little sentiment, a little promise, perhaps."

"It is not artistic," Prince Shan pronounced calmly. "It is not when the wine mounts to the head, and the sense of feeding fills the body, that men speak best of the things that lie near their hearts. Still, we will let that pass. Each of us is made differently. There is another thing, Immelan, which I have to say to you."

They passed into the reception room, with its shining floor, its marvellous rugs, its silken hangings, and its great vases of flowers. Prince Shan led his companion into a recess, where the light failed to penetrate so completely as into the rest of the apartment. A wide settee, piled with cushions, protruded from the wall in semicircular shape. In front of it was a round ebony table, upon which stood a great yellow bowl filled with lilies. Prince Shan gave an order to one of the servants who had followed them into the room and threw himself at full length among the cushions, his head resting upon his hand, his face turned towards his guest.

"They will bring you the aperitif of which you are so fond," he said, "also cigarettes. Mine, I know, are too strong for you."

"They taste too much of opium," Immelan remarked.

Prince Shan's eyes grew dreamy as he gazed through a little cloud of odorous smoke.

"There is opium in them," he admitted. "Believe me, they are very wonderful, but I agree with you that they are not for the ordinary person."

The soft-footed butler presented a silver tray, upon which reposed a glassful of amber liquid. Immelan took it, sipped it appreciatively, and lit a cigarette.

"Your man, Prince," he acknowledged, "mixes his vermouths wonderfully."

"I am glad that what he does meets with your approval," was the courteous reply. "He came to me from one of your royal palaces. I simply told him that I wished my guests to have of the best."

"Yet you never touch this sort of drink yourself," Immelan observed curiously.

The Prince shook his head.

"Sometimes I take wine," he said. "That is generally at night. A few evenings ago, for instance," he went on, with a reminiscent smile, "I drank Chateau Yquem, smoked Egyptian cigarettes, ate some muscatel grapes, and read 'Pippa Passes.' That was one of my banquets."

"As a matter of fact," Immelan remarked thoughtfully, "you are far more western in thought than in habit. The temperance of the East is in your blood."

"I find that my manner of life keeps the brain clear," Prince Shan said slowly. "I can see the truth sometimes when it is not very apparent. I saw the truth last night, Immelan, when I sent Sen Lu to die."

Immelan's expression was indescribable. He sat with his mouth wide open. The hand which held his glass shook. He stared across the bowl of lilies to where his host was looking up through the smoke towards the ceiling.

"Sen Lu was a traitor," the latter went on, "a very foolish man who with one act of treachery wiped out the memory of a lifetime of devotion. In the end he told the truth, and now he has paid his debt."

"What do you mean?" Immelan demanded, in a voice which he attempted in vain to control. "How was Sen Lu a traitor?"

"Sen Lu," the Prince explained, "was in the pay of those who sought to know more of my business than I chose to tell—who sought, indeed, to anticipate my own judgment. When they gathered from him, and, alas! from my sweet but frail little friend Nita, that the chances were against my signing a certain covenant, they came to what, even now, seems to me a strange decision. They decided that I must die. There I fail wholly to follow the workings of your mind, Immelan. How was my death likely to serve your purpose?"

Immelan was absolutely speechless. Three times he opened his lips, only to close them again. Some instinct seemed to tell him that his companion had more to say. He sat there as though mesmerised. Meanwhile, the Prince lit another cigarette.

"A blunder, believe me, Immelan," he continued thoughtfully. "Death will not lower over my path till my task is accomplished. I am young—many years younger than you, Immelan—and the greatest physicians marvel at my strength. Against the assassin's knife or bullet I am secure. You have been brought up and lived, my terrified friend, in a country where religion remains a shell and a husk, without comfort to any man. It is not so with me, I live in the spirit as in the body, and my days will last until the sun leans down and lights me to the world where those dwell who have fulfilled their destiny."

Immelan drained the contents of the glass which his unsteady hand was holding. Then he rose to his feet. The veins on his forehead were standing out, his blue eyes were filled with rage.

"Blast Sen Lu!" he muttered. "The man was a double traitor!"

"He has atoned," his companion said calmly. "He made his peace and he went to his death. It seems very fitting that he should have received the dagger which was meant for my heart. Now what about you, Oscar Immelan?"

Immelan laughed harshly.

"If Sen Lu told you that I was in this plot against your life, he lied!"

The Prince inclined his head urbanely.

"Such a man as Sen Lu goes seldom to his death with a lie upon his lips," he said. "Yet I confess that I am puzzled. Why should you plan this thing, Immelan? You cannot know what is in my mind concerning your covenant. I have not yet refused to sign it."

"You have not refused to sign it," Immelan replied, "but you will refuse."

"Indeed?" the Prince murmured.

"You are even now trifling with the secrets confided to you," Immelan went on. "You know very well that the woman who came to you last night is a spy whose whole time is spent in seeking to worm our secret from you."

"Your agents keep themselves well informed," was the calm comment.

"Yours still have the advantage of us," Immelan answered bitterly. "Now listen to me. I have heard it said of you—I have heard that you claim yourself—that you have never told a falsehood. We have been allies. Answer me this question. Have you parted with any of our secrets?"

"Not one," the Prince assured him. "A certain lady visited this house last night, not, as you seem to think, at my invitation, but on her own initiative. She was not successful in her quest."

"She would not pay the price, eh?" Immelan sneered. "By the gods of your ancestors, Prince Shan, are there not women enough in the world for you without bartering your honour, and the great future of your country, for a blue-eyed jade of an Englishwoman?"

The Prince sat slowly up. His appearance was ominous. His face had become set as marble; there was a look in his eyes like the flashing of a light upon black metal. He contemplated his visitor across the lilies.

"A man so near to death, Immelan," he enjoined, "might choose his words more carefully."

Immelan laughed scornfully.

"I am not to be bullied," he declared. "Your doors with their patent locks have no fears for me. When you walk abroad, you are followed by members of your household. When you come to my rooms, they attend you. I am not a prince, but I, too, have a care for my skin. Three of my secret service men never let me out of their sight. They are within call at this moment."

His host smiled.

"This is very interesting," he said, "but you should know me better, Immelan, than to imagine that mine are the clumsy methods of the dagger or the bullet. The man whom I will to die—drinks with me."

He pointed a long forefinger at the empty glass. Immelan gazed at it, and the sweat stood out upon his forehead.

"My God!" he muttered. "There was a queer taste! I thought that it was aniseed!"

"There was nothing in that glass," the Prince declared, "which the greatest chemist who ever breathed could detect as poison, yet you will die, my friend Immelan, without any doubt. Shall I tell you how? Would you know in what manner the pains will come? No? But, my friend, you disappoint me! You showed so much courage an hour ago. Listen. Feel for a swelling just behind—Ah!"

Immelan was already across the room. The Prince touched a bell, the doors were opened. Ghastly pale, his head swimming, the tortured man dashed out into the street. The Prince leaned back amongst his cushions, untied a straw-fastened packet of his long cigarettes, lit one, and closed his eyes.

XXVI

Nigel was just arriving at Dorminster House when Maggie returned from her ride. He assisted her to dismount and entered the house with her.

"There is something here I should like to show you, Maggie," he said, as he drew a dispatch from his pocket. "It was sent round to me half an hour ago by Chalmers, from the American Embassy."

"It's about Gilbert Jesson!" Maggie exclaimed, holding out her hand for it.

Nigel nodded.

"There's a note inside, and an enclosure," he said. "You had better read both."

Maggie opened out the former:

My Dear Dorminster,

I am afraid there is rather bad news about Jesson. One of our regular line of airships, running from San Francisco to Vladivostok, has picked up a wireless which must have come from somewhere in the South of China. They kept it for a few days, worse luck, thinking it was only nonsense, as it was in code. Washington got hold of it, however, and cabled it to us last night. I enclose a copy, decoded.

Sincerely yours,
Jere Chalmers

The copy was brief enough. Maggie felt her heart sink as she glanced through the few lines:

Report dispatched London. Fear escape impossible.

Good-by
Jesson

"Horrible!" Maggie exclaimed, with a shiver. "I thought he was in Russia."

"So did we all," Nigel replied. "He must have come to the conclusion that the key to the riddle he was trying to solve was in China, and gone on there. Look here, Maggie," he continued, after a moment's hesitation, "do you think anything could be done for Jesson with Prince Shan?"

Maggie was silent. They were standing in a shaded corner of the hall, but a fleck of sunshine shone in her hair. She was still a little out of breath with the exercise, her cheeks full of healthy colour, her eyes bright. She tapped her skirt with her riding whip. Nigel watched her a little uneasily.

"Prince Shan is calling here this afternoon," Maggie announced. "I hope you don't mind."

"What are you going to say to him?" Nigel asked bluntly.

There was a short, tense silence. Even at the thought of the crisis which she knew to be so close at hand, Maggie felt herself unnerved and in dubious straits.

"I do not know," she said at last. "For one thing, I do not know what he wants."

"What he wants seems perfectly plain to me," Nigel replied gravely. "He wants you."

Maggie made a desperate effort to regain the lightheartedness of a few weeks ago.

"If you believe that," she said, "your composure is most unflattering."

There was a ring at the front doorbell, and a familiar voice was heard outside. Maggie turned away to the staircase with a little sigh of relief.

"Naida!" she exclaimed. "I remember now I asked her for a quarter past one instead of half-past. You must entertain her, Nigel. I'll change into something quickly. And of course I'll speak to Prince Shan. We mustn't lose a minute about that. I'll telephone from my room in a few minutes, Naida. Nigel will look after you."

Naida came down the hall, cool and exquisitely gowned in a creation of shimmering white. Nigel led her into the rarely used drawing-room and found a chair for her between the open window and the conservatory. At first they exchanged but few words. The sense of her near presence affected Nigel as nothing of the sort had ever done before. She for her part seemed quite content with a silence which had in it many of the essentials of eloquence.

"If the history of these days is ever written by an irascible German historian," Naida remarked at length, "he will probably declare that the destinies of the world have been affected during this last month by an outburst of primitivism. Do you know that I have written quite nice things to Paul about you English people? Honest things, of course, but still things which you helped me to discover. And Prince Shan, too. I think that when he rode here through the clouds, he believed in his heart that he was coming as a harbinger of woe."

"You really think, then, that the crisis is past?" Nigel asked.

She nodded.

"I am almost sure of it. Prince Shan returns to China within the course of the next few days."

"We have lived so long," Nigel observed, "in dread of the unknown. I wonder whether we shall ever understand the exact nature of the danger with which we were faced."

"It depends upon Prince Shan," she replied. "The terms were Immelan's, but the method was his."

"Do you believe," he asked a little abruptly, "that the attempt on Prince Shan's life last night was made by Immelan?"

There was a touch, perhaps, of her Muscovite ancestry in the cool indifference with which she considered the matter.

"I should think it most likely," she decided. "Prince Shan never changes his mind, and I believe that he has decided against Immelan's scheme. Immelan's only chance would be in Prince Shan's successor."

"Why is China so necessary?" Nigel asked.

She turned and smiled at her companion.

"Alas!" she sighed, "we have reached an *impasse*. The great English diplomat asks too many questions of the simple Russian girl."

"It is unfortunate," he replied, in the same vein, "because I feel like asking more."

"As, for example?"

"Whether you would be content to live for the rest of your life in any other country except Russia."

"A woman is content to live anywhere, under certain circumstances," she murmured.

Karschoff, discreetly announced, entered the room with flamboyant ease.

"It is well to be young!" he exclaimed, as he bent over Naida's fingers. "You look, my far-away but much beloved cousin, as though you had slept peacefully through the night and spent the morning in this soft, sunlit air, with perhaps, if one might suggest such a thing, an hour at a Bond Street beauty parlour. Here am I with crow's-feet under my eyes and ghosts walking by my side. Yet none the less," he added, as the door opened and Maggie appeared, "looking forward to my luncheon and to hear all the news."

"There is no news," Naida declared, as the butler announced the service of the meal. "We have reached the far end of the ways. The next disclosures, if ever they are made, will come from others. At luncheon we are going to talk of the English country, the seaside, the meadows, and the quiet places. The time arrives when I weary, weary, of the brazen ticking of the clock of fate."

"I shall tell you," Nigel declared, "of a small country house I have in Devonshire. There are rough grounds stretching down to the sea and crawling up to the moors behind. My grandfather built it when he was Chancellor of England, or rather he added to an old farmhouse. He called it the House of Peace."

"My father built a house very much in the same spirit," Naida told them. "He called it after an old Turkish inscription, engraven on the front of a villa in Stamboul—'The House of Thought and Flowers.'"

Maggie smiled across the table approvingly.

"I like the conversation," she said. "Naida and I are, after all, women and sentimentalists. We claim a respite, an armistice—call it what you will. Prince Karschoff, won't you tell me of the most beautiful house you ever dwelt in?"

"Always the house I am hoping to end my days in," he answered. "But let me tell you about a villa I had in Cannes, fifteen years ago. People used to speak of it as one of the world's treasures."

When the two men were seated alone over their coffee, Nigel passed Chalmers' note and the enclosure across to his companion.

"You remember I told you about Chalmers' friend, Jesson, the secret service man who came over to us?" he said. "Chalmers has just sent me round this."

Karschoff nodded and studied the message through his great horn-rimmed eyeglass.

"I thought that he was going to Russia for you," he said.

"So he did. He must have gone on from there."

"And the message comes from Southern China," Prince Karschoff reflected.

Nigel was deep in thought. China, Russia, Germany! Prince Shan in England, negotiating with Immelan! And behind, sinister, menacing, mysterious—Japan!

"Supposing," he propounded at last, "there really does exist a secret treaty between China and Japan?"

"If there is," Prince Karschoff observed, "one can easily understand what Immelan has been at. Prince Shan can command the whole of Asia. I know they are afraid of something of the sort in the States. An American who was in the club yesterday told us they had spent over a hundred millions on their west coast fortifications in the last two years."

"One can understand, too, in that case," Nigel continued, "why Japan left the League of Nations. That stunt of hers about being outside the sphere of possible misunderstandings never sounded honest."

"It was unfortunate," Prince Karschoff said, "that America was dominated for those few months by an honest but impractical idealist. He had the germ of an idea, but he thrust it on the world before even his own country was ready for it. In time the nations would certainly have elaborated something more workable."

"You cannot keep a full-blooded man from clenching his fist if he's insulted," Nigel pointed out, "and nations march along the same lines as individuals. Its existence has never for a single moment weakened Germany's hatred of England, and the stronger she grows, the more she flaunts its conditions. France guards her frontiers, night and day, with an army ten times larger than she is allowed. Russia has become the country of mysteries, with something up her sleeve, beyond a doubt, and there are cities in modern China into which no European dare penetrate. Japan quite frankly maintains an immense army, the United States is silently following suit—and God help us all if a war does come!"

"You are right," Karschoff assented gloomily. "The last glamour of romance has gone from fighting. There were remnants of it in the last war, especially in Palestine and Egypt and when we first overran Austria. To-day, science would settle the whole affair. The war would be won in the laboratory, the engine room and the workshop. I doubt whether any battleship could keep afloat for a week, and as to the fighting in the air, if a hundred airships were in action, I do not suppose that one of them would escape. Then they say that France has a gun which could carry a shell from Amiens to London, and more mysterious than all, China has something up her sleeve which no one has even a glimmering of."

"Except Jesson," Nigel muttered.

"And Jesson's gleam of knowledge, or suspicion," Prince Karschoff remarked, "seems to have brought him to the end of his days. Can anything be done with Prince Shan about him, do you think?"

"Only indirectly, I am afraid," Nigel replied. "Maggie is seeing him this afternoon. As a matter of fact, I believe she telephoned to him before luncheon, but I haven't heard anything yet. When a man goes out on that sort of a job, he burns his boats. And Jesson isn't the first who has turned eastwards, during the last few months. I heard only yesterday that France has lost three of her best men in China—one who went as a missionary and two as merchants. They've just disappeared without a word of explanation."

The telephone extension bell rang. Nigel walked over to the sideboard and took down the receiver.

"Is that Lord Dorminster?" a man's voice asked.

"Speaking," Nigel replied.

"I am David Franklin, private secretary to Mr. Mervin Brown," the voice continued. "Mr. Mervin Brown would be exceedingly obliged if you would come round to Downing Street to see him at once."

"I will be there in ten minutes," Nigel promised.

He laid down the receiver and turned to Karschoff.

"The Prime Minister," he explained.

"What does he want you for?"

"I think," Nigel replied, "that the trouble cloud is about to burst."

XXVII

M r. Mervin Brown on this occasion did not beat about the bush. His old air of confident, almost smug self-satisfaction, had vanished. He received Nigel with a new deference in his manner, without any further sign of that good-natured tolerance accorded by a busy man to a kindly crank.

"Lord Dorminster," he began, "I have sent for you to renew a conversation we had some little time since. I will be quite frank with you. Certain circumstances have come to my notice which lead me to believe that there may be more truth in some of the arguments you brought forward than I was willing at the time to believe."

"I must confess that I am relieved to hear you say so," Nigel replied. "All the information which I have points to a crisis very near at hand."

The Prime Minister leaned a little across the table.

"The immediate reason for my sending for you," he explained, "is this. My friend the American Ambassador has just sent me a copy of a wireless dispatch which he has received from China from one of their former agents. The report seems to have been sent to him for safety, but the sender of it, of whose probity, by the by, the American Ambassador pledges himself, appears to have been sent to China by you."

"Jesson!" Nigel exclaimed. "I have heard of this already, sir, from a friend in the American Embassy."

"The dispatch," Mr. Mervin Brown went on, "is in some respects a little vague, but it is, on the other hand, I frankly admit, disturbing. It gives specific details as to definite military preparations on the part of China and Russia, associated, presumably, with a third Power whose name you will forgive my not mentioning. These preparations appear to have been brought almost to completion in the strictest secrecy, but the headquarters of the whole thing, very much to my surprise, I must confess, seems to be in southern China."

"In that case," Nigel pointed out, "if you will permit me to make a suggestion, sir, you have a very simple course open to you."

"Well?"

"Send for Prince Shan."

"Prince Shan," the Prime Minister replied, with knitted brows, "is not over in this country officially. He has begged to be excused from accepting or returning any diplomatic courtesies."

"Nevertheless," Nigel persisted, "I should send for Prince Shan. If it had not been," he went on slowly, "for the complete abolition of our secret service system, you would probably have been informed before now that Prince Shan has been having continual conferences in this country with one of the most dangerous men who ever set foot on these shores—Oscar Immelan."

"Immelan has no official position in this country," the Prime Minister objected.

"A fact which makes him none the less dangerous," Nigel insisted. "He is one of those free lances of diplomacy who have sprung up during the last ten or fifteen years, the product of that spurious wave of altruism which is responsible for the League of Nations. Immelan was one of the first to see how his country might benefit by the new régime. It is he who has been pulling the strings in Russia and China, and, I fear, another country."

"What I want to arrive at," Mr. Mervin Brown said, a little impatiently, "is something definite."

"Let me put it my own way," Nigel begged. "A very large section of our present-day politicians—you, if I may say so, amongst them, Mr. Mervin Brown—have believed this country safe against any military dangers, because of the connections existing between your unions of working men and similar bodies in Germany. This is a great fallacy for two reasons: first because Germany has always intended to have some one else pull the chestnuts out of the fire for her, and second because we cannot internationalise labour. English and German workmen may come together on matters affecting their craft and the conditions of their labour, but at heart one remains a German and one an Englishman, with separate interests and a separate outlook."

"Well, at the end of it all," Mr. Mervin Brown said, "the bogey is war. What sort of a war? An invasion of England is just as impossible to-day as it was twenty years ago."

Nigel nodded.

"I cannot answer your question," he admitted. "I was looking to Jesson's report to give us an idea as to that."

"You shall see it to-morrow," Mr. Mervin Brown promised. "It is round at the War Office at the present moment."

"Without seeing it," Nigel went on, "I expect I can tell you one startling feature of its contents. It suggested, did it not, that the principal movers against us would be Russian and China and—a country which you prefer just now not to mention?"

"But that country is our ally!" Mr. Mervin Brown exclaimed.

Nigel smiled a little sadly.

"She has been," he admitted. "Still, if you had been *au fait* with diplomatic history thirty years ago, Mr. Mervin Brown, you would know that she was on the point of ending her alliance with us and establishing one with Germany. It was only owing to the genius of one English statesman that at the last moment she almost reluctantly renewed her alliance with us. She is in the same state of doubt concerning our destiny to-day. She has seen our last two Governments forget that we are an Imperial Power and endeavour to apply the principles of sheer commercialism to the conduct of a great nation. She may have opened her eyes a thousand years later than we did, but she is awake enough now to know that this will not do. There is little enough of generosity amongst the nations; none amongst the Orientals. I have a conviction myself that there is a secret alliance between China and this other Power, a secret and quite possibly an aggressive alliance."

Mr. Mervin Brown sat for a few moments deep in thought. Somehow or other his face had gained in dignity since the beginning of the conversation. The nervous fear in his eyes had been replaced by a look of deep and solemn anxiety.

"If you are right, Lord Dorminster," he pronounced presently, "the world has rolled backwards these last ten years, and we who have failed to mark its retrogression may have a terrible responsibility thrust upon us."

"Politically, I am afraid I agree with you," Nigel replied. "Only the idealist, and the prejudiced idealist, can ignore the primal elements in human nature and believe that a few lofty sentiments can keep the nations behind their frontiers. War is a terrible thing, but human life itself is a terrible thing. Its principles are the same, and force will never be restrained except by force. If the League of Nations had been established upon a firmer and less selfish basis, it certainly might have kept the peace for another thirty or forty years. As it is, I believe that we are on the verge of a serious crisis."

"War for us is an impossibility," Mr. Mervin Brown declared frankly, "simply because we cannot fight. Our army consists of policemen; science has defeated the battleship; and practically the same conditions exist in the air."

"You sent for me, I presume, to ask for my advice," Nigel said. "At any rate, let me offer it. I have reason to believe that the negotiations between Prince Shan and Oscar Immelan have not been entirely successful. Send for Prince Shan and question him in a friendly fashion."

"Will you be my ambassador?" the Prime Minister asked.

Nigel hesitated for a moment.

"If you wish it," he promised. "Prince Shan is in some respects a strangely inaccessible person, but just at present he seems well disposed towards my household."

"Arrange, if you can," Mr. Mervin Brown begged, "to bring him here to-morrow morning. I will try to have available a copy of the dispatch from Jesson. It refers to matters which I trust Prince Shan will be able to explain."

Nigel lingered for a moment over his farewell.

"If I might venture upon a suggestion, sir," he said, "do not forget that Prince Shan is to all intents and purposes the autocrat of Asia. He has taught the people of the world to remodel their ideas of China and all that China stands for. And further than this, he is, according to his principles, a man of the strictest honour. I would treat him, sir, as a valued *confrère* and equal."

The Prime Minister smiled.

"Don't look upon me as being too intensely parochial, Dorminster," he said. "I know quite well that Prince Shan is a man of genius, and that he is a representative of one of the world's greatest families. I am only the servant of a great Power. He is a great Power in himself."

"And believe me," Nigel concluded fervently, as he made his adieux, "the greatest autocrat that ever breathed. If, when you exchange farewells with him, he says—'There will be no war'—we are saved, at any rate for the moment."

XXVIII

Maggie, very cool and neat, a vision of soft blue, a wealth of colouring in the deep brown of her closely braided hair, her lips slightly parted in a smile of welcome, felt, notwithstanding her apparent composure, a strange disturbance of outlook and senses as Prince Shan was ushered into her flower-bedecked little sitting room that afternoon. The unusual formality of his entrance seemed somehow to suit the man and his manner. He bowed low as soon as he had crossed the threshold and bowed again over her fingers as she rose from her easy-chair.

"It makes me very happy that you receive me like this," he told her simply. "It makes it so much easier for me to say the things that are in my heart."

"Won't you sit down, please?" Maggie invited. "You are so tall, and I hate to be completely dominated."

He obeyed at once, but he continued to talk with grave and purposeful seriousness.

"I wish," he said, "to bring myself entirely into accord, for these few minutes, with your western methods and customs. I address you, therefore, Lady Maggie, with formal words, while I keep back in my heart much that is struggling to express itself. I have come to ask you to do me the great honour of becoming my wife."

Maggie sat for a few moments speechless. The thing which she had half dreaded and half longed for—the low timbre of his caressing voice—was entirely absent. Yet, somehow or other, his simple, formal words were at least as disturbing. He leaned towards her, a quiet, dignified figure, anxious yet in a sense confident. He had the air of a man who has offered to share a kingdom.

"Your wife," Maggie repeated tremulously.

"The thought is new to you, perhaps," he went on, with gentle tolerance. "You have believed the stories people tell that in my youth I was vowed to celibacy and the priesthood. That is not true. I have always been free to marry, but although to-day we figure as a great progressive nation, many of the thousand-year-old ideas of ancient China have dwelt in my brain and still sit enshrined in my heart. The aristocracy of China has passed through evil times. There is no princess of my own country whom I could meet on equal terms. So, you see, although it develops differently, there is something of the snobbishness of your western countries reflected in our own ideas."

"But I am not a princess," Maggie murmured.

"You are the princess of my soul," he answered, lowering his eyes for a moment almost reverently. "I cannot quite hope to make you understand, but if I took for my wife a Chinese lady of unequal mundane rank, I should commit a serious offence against those who watch me from the other side of the grave, and to whom I am accountable for every action of my life. A lady of another country is a different matter."

"But I am an Englishwoman," Maggie said, "and I love my country. You know what that means."

"I know very well," he admitted. "I had not meant to speak of those things until later, but, for your country's sake, what greater alliance could you seek to-day than to become the wife of him who is destined to be the Ruler of Asia?"

Maggie caught hold of her courage. She looked into his eyes unflinchingly, though she felt the hot colour rise into her cheeks.

"You did not speak to me of these things, Prince Shan, when I came to your house last night," she reminded him.

His smile was full of composure. It was as though the truth which sat enshrined in the man's soul lifted him above all the ordinary emotions of fear of misunderstandings.

"For those few minutes," he confessed, "I was very angry. It brings great pain to a man to see the thing he loves droop her wings, flutter down to earth, and walk the common highway. It is not for you, dear one, to mingle with that crowd who scheme and cheat, hide and deceive, for any reward in the world, whether it be money, fame, or the love of country. You were not made for those things, and when I saw you there, so utterly in my power, having deliberately taken your risk, I was angry. For a single moment I meant that you should realise the danger of the path you were treading. I think that I did make you realise it."

Her eyes fell. He seemed to have established some compelling power over her. He had met her thoughts before they were uttered, and answered even her unspoken question.

"I wish you didn't make life so much like a kindergarten," she complained, with an almost pathetic smile at the corners of her lips.

"It is a very different place," he rejoined fervently, "that I desire to make of life for you. Listen, please. I have spoken to you first the formal words which make all things possible between us, and now, if

I may, I let my heart speak. Somewhere not far from Pekin I have a palace, where my lands slope to the river. For five months in the year my gardens are starred with blue and yellow flowers, sweet-smelling as the almond blossom, and there are little pagodas which look down on the blue water, pagodas hung with creepers, not like your English evergreens, but with blossoms, pink and waxen, which open as one looks at them and send out sweet perfumes. When you are there with me, dear one, then I shall speak to you in the language of my ancestors, which some day you will understand, and you shall know that love has its cradle in the East, you shall feel the flame of its birth, the furnace of its accomplishment. Here my tongue moves slowly, yet I stoop my knee to you, I show you my heart, and my lips tell you that I love. What that love is you shall learn some day, if you have the will and the confidence and the soul. Will you come back to China with me, Maggie?"

She rested her fingers on his hand.

"You are a magician," she confessed. "I am very English, and yet I want to go."

He stood for a moment looking into her eyes. Then he stooped down and raised her hesitating fingers to his lips.

"I believe that you will come," he said simply. "I believe that you will ride over the clouds with me, back to the country of beautiful places. So now I speak to you of serious things. Of money there shall be what you wish, more than any woman even of your rank possesses in this country. I shall give you, too, the sister of my great *Black Dragon* so that in five days, if you wish, you can pass from any of my palaces to London. And further than that, behold!"

He drew from his pocket a roll of papers. Maggie recognised it, and her heart beat faster. Curiously enough, just then she scarcely thought of its world importance. She remembered only those few moments of strange thrills, the wonder at finding him in that room, as he stood watching her, the horror and yet the thrill of his measured words. He laid the papers upon the table.

"Read them," he invited. "You will understand then the net that has been closing around your country. You will understand the better if I tell you this. China and Japan are one. It was my first triumph when patriotism urged me into the field of politics. We have a single motto, and upon that is based all that you may read there,—'*Europe for the Europeans, Asia for us.*'"

Maggie was conscious of a sudden sense of escape from her almost mesmeric state. The change in his tone, his calm references to things belonging to another and altogether different world, had dissolved a situation against the charm of which she had found herself powerless, even unwilling to struggle. Once more she was back in the world where for the last two years had lain her chief interests. She took the papers in her hand and began reading them quickly through. Every now and then a little exclamation broke from her lips.

"You will observe," her companion pointed out, looking over her shoulder, "that on paper, at any rate, Japan is the great gainer. She takes Australia, New Zealand and India. China absorbs Thibet and reëstablishes her empire of forty years ago. The arrangement is based very largely on racial conditions. China is a self-centered country. We have not the power of fusion of the Japanese. You will observe further, as an interesting circumstance, that the American foothold in Asia disappears as completely as the British."

"But tell me," she demanded, "how are these things to be brought about, and where does Immelan come in?"

Prince Shan smiled.

"Immelan's position," he explained, "is largely a sentimental one, yet on the other hand he saves his country from what might be a grave calamity. The commercial advantages he gains under this treaty might seem to be inadequate, although in effect they are very considerable. The point is this. He soothes his country of the pain which groans day by day in her limbs. He gratifies her lust for vengeance against Great Britain without plunging her into any desperate enterprise."

"And France escapes," she murmured.

"France escapes," he assented. "Rightly or wrongly, the whole of Germany's post-war animosity was directed against England. She considered herself deceived by certain British statesmen. She may have been right or wrong. I myself find the evidence conflicting. At this moment the matter does not concern us."

"And is Great Britain, then," Maggie asked, "believed to be so helpless that she can be stripped of the greater part of her possessions at the will of China and Japan?"

Prince Shan smiled.

"Great Britain," he reminded her, "has taken the League of Nations to her heart. It was a very dangerous thing to do."

"Still," Maggie persisted, "there remains the great thing which you have not told me. These proposals, I admit, would strike a blow at the heart of the British Empire, but how are they to be carried into effect?"

"If I had signed the agreement," he replied, "they could very easily have been carried into effect. You have heard already, have you not, through some of your agents, of the three secret cities? In the eastern-most of them is the answer to your question."

She smiled.

"Is that a challenge to me to come out and discover for myself all that I want to know?"

"If you come," he answered, "you shall certainly know everything. There is another little matter, too, which waits for your decision."

"Tell me of it at once, please," she begged, with a sudden conviction of his meaning.

He obeyed without hesitation.

"I spoke just now," he reminded her, "of the three secret cities. They are secret because we have taken pains to keep them so. One is in Germany, one in Russia, and one in China. A casual traveller could discover little in the German one, and little more, perhaps, in the Russian one. Enough to whet his curiosity, and no more. But in China there is the whole secret at the mercy of a successful spy. A man named Jesson, Lady Maggie—"

"I telephoned you about him before luncheon to-day," she interrupted.

"I had your message," he replied, "and the man is safe for the moment. At the same time, Lady Maggie, let me remind you that this is a game the rules of which are known the world over. Jesson has now in his possession the secret on which I might build, if I chose, plans to conquer the world. He knew the penalty if he was discovered, and he was discovered. To spare his life is sentimentalism pure and simple, yet if it is your will, so be it."

"You are very good to me," she declared gratefully, "all the more good because half the time I can see that you scarcely understand."

"That I do not admit," he protested. "I understand even where I do not sympathise. You make of life the greatest boon on earth. We of my race and way of thinking are taught to take it up or lay it down, if not with indifference, at any rate with a very large share of resignation. However, Jesson's life is spared. From what I have heard of the man, I imagine he will be very much surprised."

She gave a little sigh of relief.

"You have given me a great deal of your confidence," she said thoughtfully.

"Is it not clear," he answered, "why I have done so? I ask of you the greatest boon a woman has to give. I do not seek to bribe, but if you can give me the love that will make my life a dream of happiness, then will it not be my duty to see that no shadow of misfortune shall come to you or yours? China stands between Japan and Russia, and I am China."

She gave him her hands.

"You are very wonderful," she declared. "Remember that at a time like this, it is not a woman's will alone that speaks. It is her soul which lights the way. Prince Shan, I do not know."

He smiled gravely.

"I leave," he told her, "on Friday, soon after dawn."

She found herself trembling.

"It is a very short time," she faltered.

They had both risen to their feet. He was close to her now, and she felt herself caught up in a passionate wave of inertia, an absolute inability to protest or resist. His arms were clasped around her lightly and with exceeding gentleness. He leaned down. She found herself wondering, even in that tumultuous moment, at the strange clearness of his complexion, the whiteness of his firm, strong teeth, the soft brilliance of his eyes, which caressed her even before his lips rested upon hers.

"I think that you will come," he whispered. "I think that you will be very happy."

XXIX

The great house in Curzon Street awoke, the following morning, to a state of intense activity. Taxi-cabs and motor-cars were lined along the street; a stream of callers came and went. That part of the establishment of which little was seen by the casual caller, the rooms where half a dozen secretaries conducted an immense correspondence, presided over by Li Wen, was working overtime at full pressure. In his reception room, Prince Shan saw a selected few of the callers, mostly journalists and politicians, to whom Li Wen gave the entrée. One visitor even this most astute of secretaries found it hard to place. He took the card in to his master, who glanced at it thoughtfully.

"The Earl of Dorminster," he repeated. "I will see him."

Nigel found himself received with courtesy, yet with a certain aloofness. Prince Shan rose from his favourite chair of plain black oak heaped with green silk cushions and held out his hand a little tentatively.

"You are very kind to visit me, Lord Dorminster," he said. "I trust that you come to wish me fortune."

"That," Nigel replied, "depends upon how you choose to seek it."

"I am answered," was the prompt acknowledgment. "One thing in your country I have at least learnt to appreciate, and that is your love of candour. What is your errand with me to-day? Have you come to speak to me as an ambassador from your cousin, or in any way on her behalf?"

"My business has nothing to do with Lady Maggie," Nigel assured him gravely.

Prince Shan held out his hand.

"Stop," he begged. "Do not explain your business. If it is a personal request, it is granted. If, on the other hand, you seek my advice on matters of grave importance, it is yours. Before other words are spoken, however, I myself desire to address you on the subject of Lady Maggie Trent."

"As you please," Nigel answered.

"It is not the custom of my country, or of my life," Prince Shan continued, "to covet or steal the things which belong to another. If fate has made me a thief, I am very sorry. I have proposed to Lady Maggie that she accompany me back to China. It is my great desire that she should become my wife."

Nigel felt himself curiously tongue-tied. There was something in the other's measured speech, so fateful, so assured, that it seemed almost as though he were speaking of pre-ordained things. Much that had seemed to him impossible and unnatural in such an idea disappeared from that moment.

"You tell me this," Nigel began—

"I announce it to you as the head of the family," Prince Shan interrupted.

"You tell it to me also," Nigel persisted, "because you have heard the rumours which were at one time very prevalent—that Lady Maggie and I were or were about to become engaged to be married."

"I have heard such a rumour only very indirectly," Prince Shan confessed, "and I cannot admit that it has made any difference in my attitude. I think, in my land and yours, we have at least one common convention. The woman who touches our heart is ours if we may win her. Love is unalterably selfish. One must fight for one's own hand. And for those who may suffer by our victory, we may have pity but no consideration."

"Am I to understand," Nigel asked bluntly, "that Lady Maggie has consented to be your wife?"

"Lady Maggie has given me no reply. I left her alone with her thoughts. Every hour it is my hope to hear from her. She knows that I leave for China early to-morrow."

"So at the present moment you are in suspense."

"I am in suspense," Prince Shan admitted, "and perhaps," he went on, with one of his rare smiles, "it occurred to me that it would be in one sense a relief to speak to a fellow man of the hopes and fears that are in my heart. You are the one person to whom I could speak, Lord Dorminster. You have not wished my suit well, but at least you have been clear-sighted. I think it has never occurred to you that a prince of China might venture to compete with a peer of England."

"On the contrary," Nigel assented, "I have the greatest admiration for the few living descendants of the world's oldest aristocracy. You have a right to enter the lists, a right to win if you can."

"And what do you think of my prospects, if I may ask such a delicate question?" Prince Shan enquired.

"I cannot estimate them," Nigel replied. "I only know that Maggie is deeply interested."

"I think," his companion continued softly, "that she will become my Princess. You have never visited China, Lord Dorminster," he went on, "so you have little idea, perhaps, as to the manner of our lives. Some day I will hope to be your host, so until then, as I may not speak of my own possessions, may I go just so far as this? Your cousin will be very happy in China. This is a great country, but the very air you breathe is cloyed with your national utilitarianism. Mine is a country of beautiful thoughts, of beautiful places, of quiet-living and sedate people. I can give your cousin every luxury of which the world has ever dreamed, wrapped and enshrined in beauty. No person with a soul could be unhappy in the places where she will dwell."

"You are at least confident," Nigel remarked.

"It is because I am convinced," was the calm rejoinder. "I shall take your cousin's happiness into my keeping without one shadow of misgiving. The last word, however, is with her. It remains to be seen whether her courage is great enough to induce her to face such a complete change in the manner of her life."

"It will not be her lack of courage which will keep her in England," Nigel declared.

Prince Shan bowed, with a graceful little gesture of the hands. The subject was finished.

"I shall now, Lord Dorminster," he said, "take advantage of your kindly presence here to speak to you on a very personal matter, only this time it is you who are the central figure, and I who am the dummy."

"I do not follow you," Nigel confessed, with a slight frown.

"I speak in tones of apology," Prince Shan went on, "but you must remember that I am one of reflective disposition; Nature has endowed me with some of the gifts of my great ancestors, philosophers famed the world over. It seems very clear to me that, if I had not come, from sheer force of affectionate propinquity you would have married Lady Maggie."

Nigel's frown deepened.

"Prince Shan!" he began.

Again the outstretched hand seemed as though the fingers were pressed against his mouth. He broke off abruptly in his protest.

"You would have lived a contented life, because that is your province," his companion continued. "You would have felt yourself happy because you would have been a faithful husband. But the time would have come when you would both have realised that you had missed the great things."

"This is idle prophecy," Nigel observed, a little impatiently. "I came to see you upon another matter."

"Humour me," the Prince begged. "I am going to speak to you even more intimately. I shall venture to do so because, after all, she is better known to me than to you. I am going to tell you that of all the women in the world, Naida Karetsky is the most likely to make you happy."

Nigel drew himself up a little stiffly.

"One does not discuss these things," he muttered.

"May I call that a touch of insularity?" Prince Shan pleaded, "because there is nothing else in the world so wonderful to discuss, in all respect and reverence, as the women who have made us feel. One last word, Lord Dorminster. The days of matrimonial alliances between the reigning families of Europe have come to an end under the influence of a different form of government, but there is a certain type of alliance, the utility of which remains unimpaired. I venture to say that you could not do your country a greater service, apart from any personal feelings you might have, than by marrying Mademoiselle Karetsky. There, you see, now I have finished. This is for your reflection, Lord Dorminster—just the measured statement of one who wears at least the cloak of philosophy by inheritance. Time passes. Your own reason for coming to see me has not yet been expounded."

"I have come to ask you to visit the Prime Minister before you leave England," Nigel announced.

Prince Shan changed his position slightly. His forehead was a little wrinkled. He was silent for a moment.

"If I pay more than a farewell visit of ceremony," he said, "that is to say, if I speak with Mr. Mervin Brown on things that count, I must anticipate a certain decision at which I have not yet wholly arrived."

Nigel had a sudden inspiration.

"You are seeking to bribe Maggie!" he exclaimed.

"That is not true," was the dignified reply.

"Then please explain," Nigel persisted.

Prince Shan rose to his feet. He walked to the heavy silk curtains which led into his own bedchamber, pushed them apart, and looked for a moment at the familiar objects in the room. Then he came back, glancing on his way at the ebony cabinet.

"One does not repeat one's mistakes," he said slowly, "and although you and I, Lord Dorminster, breathe the common air of the greater world, my instinct tells me that of certain things which have passed between your cousin and myself it is better that no mention ever be made. I wish to tell you this, however. There is in existence a document, my signature to which would, without a doubt, have a serious influence upon the destinies of this country. That document, unsigned, would be one of my marriage gifts to Lady Maggie—and as you know I have not yet had her answer. However, if you wish it, I will go to the Prime Minister."

Li Wen came silently in. He spoke to his master for a few minutes in Chinese. A faint smile parted the latter's lips.

"You can tell the person at the telephone that I will call within the next few minutes," he directed. "You will not object," he added, turning courteously to Nigel, "if I stop for a moment, on the way to Downing Street, at a small private hospital? An acquaintance of mine lies sick there and desires urgently to see me."

"I am entirely at your service," Nigel assured him.

Prince Shan, with many apologies, left Nigel alone in the car outside a tall, grey house in John Street, and, preceded by the white-capped nurse who had opened the door, climbed the stairs to the first floor of the celebrated nursing home, where, after a moment's delay, he was shown into a large and airy apartment. Immelan was in bed, looking very ill indeed. He was pale, and his china-blue eyes, curiously protruding, were filled with an expression of haunting fear. A puzzled doctor was standing by the bedside. A nurse, who was smoothing the bedclothes, glanced around at Prince Shan's entrance. The invalid started convulsively, and, clutching the pillows with his right hand, turned towards his visitor.

"So you've come!" he exclaimed. "Stay where yon are! Don't go! Doctor—nurse—leave us alone for a moment."

The nurse went at once. The doctor hesitated.

"My patient is a good deal exhausted," he said. "There are no dangerous symptoms at present, but—"

"I will promise not to distress him," Prince Shan interrupted. "I am myself somewhat pressed for time, and it is probable that your patient will insist upon speaking to me in private."

The doctor followed the nurse from the room. Prince Shan stood looking down upon the figure of quondam associate. There was a leaven of mild wonder in his clear eyes, a faintly contemptuous smile about the corners of his lips.

"So you are afraid of death, my friend," he observed, "afraid of the death you planned so skilfully for me."

"It is a lie!" Immelan declared excitedly. "Sen Lu was never killed by my orders. Listen! You have nothing against me. My death can do you no good. It is you who have been at fault. You—Prince Shan—the great diplomatist of the world—are gambling away your future and the future of a mighty empire for a woman's sake. You have treated me badly enough. Spare my life. Call in the doctor here and tell him what to do. He can find nothing in my system. He is helpless."

The smile upon the Prince's lips became vaguer, his expression more bland and indeterminate.

"My dear Immelan," he murmured, "you are without doubt delirious. Compose yourself, I beg."

A light that was almost tragic shone in the man's face. He sat up with a sudden access of strength.

"For the love of God, don't torture me!" he groaned. "The pains grow worse, hour by hour. If I die, the whole world shall know by whose hand."

The expression on Prince Shan's face remained unchanged. In his eyes, however, there was a little glint of something which seemed almost like foreknowledge,

"When you die," he pronounced calmly, "it will be by your own hand—not mine."

For some reason or other, Immelan accepted these measured words of prophecy as a total reprieve. The relief in his face was almost piteous. He seized his visitor's hand and would have fawned upon it. Prince Shan withdrew himself a little farther from the bed.

"Immelan," he said, "during my stay in England I have studied you and your methods, I have listened to all you have had to say and to propose, I have weighed the advantages and the disadvantages of the scheme you have outlined to me, and I only arrived at my decision after the most serious and unbiassed reflection. Your scheme itself was bold and almost splendid, but, as you yourself well know at the back of your mind, it would lay the seeds of a world tumult. I have studied history, Immelan, perhaps a little more deeply than you, and I do not believe in conquests. For the restoration to China of such lands as belong geographically and rightly to the Chinese Empire, I have my own plans. You, it seems to me, would make a cat's-paw of all Asia to gratify your hatred of England."

"A cat's-paw!" Immelan gasped. "Australia, New Zealand and India for Japan, new lands for her teeming population; Thibet for you, all Manchuria, and the control of the Siberian Railway!"

"These are dazzling propositions," Prince Shan admitted, "and yet— what about the other side of the Pacific?"

"America would be powerless," Immelan insisted.

"So you said before, in 1917," was the dry reminder. "I did not come here, however, to talk world politics with you. Those things for the moment are finished. I came in answer to your summons."

Immelan raised himself a little in the bed.

"You meant what you said?" he demanded, with hoarse anxiety. "There was no poison? Swear that?"

Prince Shan moved towards the door. His backward glance was coldly contemptuous.

"What I said, I meant," he replied. "Extract such comfort from it as you may."

He left the room, closing the door softly behind him. Immelan stared after him, hollow-eyed and anxious. Already the cold fears were seizing upon him once more.

Prince Shan rejoined Nigel, and the two men drove off to Downing Street. The former was silent for the first few minutes. Then he turned slightly towards his companion.

"The man Immelan is a coward," he declared. "It is he whom I have just visited."

Nigel shrugged his shoulders.

"So many men are brave enough in a fight," he remarked, "who lose their nerve on a sick bed."

"Bravery in battle," Prince Shan pronounced, "is the lowest form of courage. The blood is stirred by the excitement of slaughter as by alcohol. With Immelan I shall have no more dealings."

"Speaking politically as well as personally?" Nigel enquired.

The other smiled.

"I think I might go so far as to agree," he acquiesced, "but in a sense, there are conditions. You shall hear what they are. I will speak before you to the Prime Minister. See, up above is the sign of my departure."

Out of a little bank of white, fleecy clouds which hung down, here and there, from the blue sky, came the *Black Dragon*, her engines purring softly, her movements slow and graceful. Both men watched her for a moment in silence.

"At six o'clock to-morrow morning I start," Prince Shan announced. "My pilot tells me that the weather conditions are wonderful, all the way from here to Pekin. We shall be there on Wednesday."

"You travel alone?" Nigel enquired.

"I have passengers," was the quiet reply. "I am taking the English chaplain to your Church in Pekin."

The eyes of the two men met.

"It is an ingenious idea," Nigel admitted dryly.

"I wish to be prepared," his companion answered. "It may be that he is my only companion. In that case, I go back to a life lonelier than I have ever dreamed of. It is on the knees of the gods. So far there has come no word, but although I am not by nature an optimist, my superstitions are on my side. All the way over on my last voyage, when I lay in my berth, awake and we sailed over and through the clouds, my star, my own particular star, seemed leaning always down towards me, and for that reason I have faith."

Nigel glanced at his companion curiously but without speech. The car pulled up in Downing Street. The two men descended and found everything made easy for them. In two minutes they were in the presence of the Prime Minister.

XXX

Mr. Mervin Brown was at his best in the interview to which he had, as a matter of fact, been looking forward with much trepidation. He received Prince Shan courteously and reproached him for not having paid him an earlier visit. To the latter's request that Nigel might be permitted to be present at the discussion, he promptly acquiesced.

"Lord Dorminster and I have already had some conversation," he said, "bearing upon the matter about which I desire to talk to you."

"I have found his lordship," Prince Shan declared, "one of the few Englishmen who has any real apprehension of the trend of events outside his own country."

The Prime Minister plunged at once into the middle of things.

"Our national faults are without doubt known to you, Prince Shan," he said. "They include, amongst other things, an over-confidence in the promises of others; too great belief, I fear, in the probity of our friends. We paid a staggering price in 1914 for those qualities. Lord Dorminster would have me believe that there is a still more terrible price for us to pay in the future, unless we change our whole outlook, abandon our belief in the League of Nations, and once more acknowledge the supremacy of force."

"Lord Dorminster is right," Prince Shan pronounced. "I have come here to tell you so, Mr. Mervin Brown."

"You come here as a friend of England?" the latter asked.

"I come here as one who hesitates to become her enemy," was the measured reply. "I will be perfectly frank with you, sir. I came to this country to discuss a project which, with the acquiescence of China and Japan, would have resulted in the humiliation of your country and the gratification of Germany's eagerly desired revenge."

"You believe in the existence of that sentiment, then?" the Prime Minister enquired.

"Any one short of a very insular Englishman," the Prince replied, "would have realised it long ago. There is a great society in Germany, scarcely even a secret society, pledged to wipe out the humiliations of the last great war. Lord Dorminster tells me that you are to-day without a secret service. For that reason you have remained in ignorance of the mines beneath your feet. Germany has laid her plans well and carefully. Her first and greatest weapon has been your sense of security. She has seen you contemplate with an ill-advised smile of spurious satisfaction, invincible France, regaining her wealth more slowly than you for the simple reason that half the man power of the country is absorbed by her military preparations. France is impregnable. A direct invasion of your country is in all probability impossible. Those two facts have seemed to you all-sufficient. That is where you have been, if I may say so, sir, very short-sighted."

"Germany has no power to transport troops in other directions," Mr. Mervin Brown observed.

Prince Shan smiled.

"You have another enemy besides Germany," he pointed out, "a great democracy who has never forgiven your lack of sympathy at her birth, your attempts to repress by force a great upheaval, borne in agony and shame, yet containing the germs of worthy things which your statesmen in those days failed to discern. Russia has never forgiven. Russia stands hand in hand with Germany."

"But surely," the Prime Minister protested, "you speak in the language of the past? The League of Nations still exists. Any directly predatory expedition would bring the rest of the world to arms."

Prince Shan shook his head.

"One of the first necessities of a tribunal," he expounded, "is that that tribunal should have the power to punish. You yourself are one of the judges. You might find your culprit guilty. With what weapon will you chastise him? The culprit has grown mightier than the judge."

"America—"

"America," Prince Shan interrupted, "can, when she chooses, strike a weightier blow than any other nation on earth, but she will never again proceed outside her own sphere of influence."

"But she must protect her trade," the Prime Minister insisted.

"She has no need to do so by force of arms. Take my own country, for instance. We need American machinery, American goods, locomotives and mining plants. America has no need to force these things upon us. We are as anxious to buy as she is to sell."

"I am to figure to myself, then," Mr. Mervin Brown reflected, "a combination of Germany and Russia engaged in some scheme inimical to Great Britain?"

"There was such a scheme definitely arranged and planned," Prince Shan assured him gravely. "If I had seen well to sign a certain paper, you would have lost, before the end of this month, India, your great treasure

　　　　　　　　　　　　　　　　　　E. PHILLIPS OPPENHEIM

house, Australia and New Zealand, and eventually Egypt. You would have been as powerless to prevent it as either of us three would be if called upon unarmed to face the champion heavyweight boxer."

"It is hard for me to credit the fact that officially Germany has any knowledge of this scheme," the Prime Minister confessed.

"Official Germany would probably deny it," Prince Shan answered dryly. "Official Russia might do the same. Official China would follow suit, but the real China, in my person, assures you of the truth of what I have told you. You have never heard, I suppose, of the three secret cities?"

"I have heard stories about them which sounded like fairy tales," Mr. Mervin Brown admitted grudgingly.

"Nevertheless, they exist," Prince Shan continued, "and they exist for the purpose of supplying means of offence for the expedition of which I have spoken. There is one in Germany, one in Russia, and one in China. The three between them have produced enough armoured airships of a new design to conquer any country in the world."

"Armoured airships?" Mr. Mervin Brown repeated.

"Airships from which one fights on land as well as in the air," Prince Shan explained. "On land they become moving fortresses. No shell has ever been made which can destroy them. I should be revealing no secret to you, because I believe I am right in saying, sir, that a model of these amazing engines of destruction was first submitted to your Government."

"I remember something of the sort," the Prime Minister assented. "The inventor himself was an American, I believe."

"Precisely! I believe he told you in plain words that whoever possessed his model might, if they chose, dominate the world."

"But who wants to dominate the world by force?" Mr. Mervin Brown demanded passionately. "We have passed into a new era, an era of peace and the higher fellowship. It is waste of time, labour and money to create these horrible instruments of destruction. The League of Nations has decreed that they shall not be built."

"Nevertheless," Prince Shan declared, with portentous gravity, "a thousand of these engines of destruction are now ready in a certain city of China. Each one of the three secret cities has done its quota of work in the shape of providing parts. China alone has put them together. I bought the secret, and I alone possess it. It rests with me whether the world remains at peace or moves on to war."

"You cannot hesitate, then?" Mr. Mervin Brown exclaimed anxiously. "You yourself are an apostle of civilisation."

Prince Shan smiled.

"It is because we are strong," he said, "that we love peace. It is because you are weak that you fear war. I am not here to teach you statesmanship. It is not for me to point out to you the means by which you can make your country safe and keep her people free. Call a meeting of what remains of the League of Nations and compare your strength with that of the nations who have crept outside and lie waiting. Then take the advice of experts and set your house in order. You sacrifice everything to-day to the god of commerce. Take a few men like Dorminster here into your councils. You are not a nation of fools. Speak the truth at the next meeting of the League of Nations and see that it is properly reported. Help yourselves, and I will help you."

"Will you come into my Cabinet, Lord Dorminster?" the Prime Minister invited, turning to Nigel.

"If you will recreate the post of Minister for War, I will do so with pleasure," was the prompt reply.

Prince Shan held out his hand.

"There is great responsibility upon your shoulders, Mr. Mervin Brown," he said. "You will never know how near you have been to disaster. Try and wake up your nation gradually, if you can. Call together your writers, your thinking men, your historians. Encourage the flagging spirit of patriotism in your public schools and universities. Is this presumption on my part that I give so much advice? If so, forgive me. Truth that sits in the heart will sometimes demand to be heard."

At the Prime Minister's request, Nigel remained behind. They both looked at the door through which Prince Shan had passed. Mr. Mervin Brown metaphorically pinched himself. He was still feeling a little dazed.

"Is that man real flesh and blood?" he demanded.

"He is as real and as near the truth," Nigel replied solemnly, "as the things of which he has told us."

XXXI

That night, Nigel gave a dinner party on Maggie's account at the fashionable London hotel of the moment. Invitations had been sent out by telephone, by hurried notes, in one or two cases were delivered by word of mouth. On the whole, the acceptances, considering the season was in full swing, were a little remarkable. Every one was anxious to come, because, as one of her girl friends put it, no one ever knew what Maggie was going to be up to next. One of the few refusals came from Prince Shan, and even he made use of compromise:

> *My dear Lord Dorminster, will you forgive me if in this instance I do not break a custom to which I have perhaps a little too rigidly adhered. The Prime Minister telephoned, a few minutes after we left him, asking me to meet two of his colleagues from the Foreign Office to-night, and I doubt whether our conference will have concluded at the hour you name.*
>
> *However, if you will permit me, I will give myself the pleasure of joining you later in the evening, to make my adieux to those of my friends whom I am quite sure I shall find amongst your company.*
>
> *Sincerely yours,*
Shan

Maggie passed the note back with a little smile. She made no comment whatever. Nigel watched her thoughtfully.

"I have carried out your orders," he observed. "Everything has been attended to, even to the colour of your table decorations. Now tell me what it all means?"

She looked him in the face quite frankly.

"How can I?" she answered. "I do not know myself."

"Is this by way of being a farewell party?" he persisted.

"I do not know that," she assured him. "The only thing is that if I do decide—to go—well, I shall have had a last glimpse of most of my friends."

"As your nearest male relative, in fact your guardian," Nigel went on, with a touch of his old manner, "I feel myself deeply interested in your present situation. If a little advice from one who is considerably your senior would be acceptable—"

"It wouldn't," Maggie interrupted quietly. "There are just two things in life no girl accepts advice upon—the way she does her hair and the man she means to marry. You see, both are decided by instinct. I shall know before dawn to-morrow what I mean to do, but until then nothing that anybody could say would make any difference. Besides, your mind ought to be full of your own matrimonial affairs. I hear that Naida is talking of going back to Russia next week."

"My own affairs are less complex," Nigel replied. "I am going to ask Naida to marry me—to-night if I have the opportunity."

Maggie made a little grimace.

"There goes my second string!" she exclaimed. "Nigel, you are horribly callous. I have never been in the least sure that I haven't wanted to marry you myself."

Nigel lit a cigarette and pushed the box across to his companion.

"I've frequently felt the same way," he confessed. "The trouble of it is that when the really right person comes along, one hasn't any doubt about it whatever. I should have made you a stodgy husband, Maggie."

She sniffed.

"I think that considering the way you've flirted with me," she declared, "you ought at least to have given me the opportunity of refusing you."

"If Naida refuses me," he began—

"And I decide that Asia is too far away," she interrupted—

"We may come together, after all," he said, with a resigned little sigh.

"Glib tongue and empty heart," she quoted. "Nigel, I would never trust you. I believe you're in love with Naida."

"And I'm not quite so sure about you," he observed, watching the colour rise quickly in her cheeks. "Off with you to dress, young woman. It's past seven, and we must be there early. I still have the wine to order."

The dinner party was in its way a complete success. Prince Karschoff was there, benign and distinguished; Chalmers and one or two other young men from the American Embassy. There was a sprinkling of Maggie's girl friends, a leaven of the older world in Nigel's few intimates,—and Naida, very pale but more beautiful than ever in a white velvet gown, her hair brushed straight back, and with no jewellery save one long rope of pearls. Nigel who in his capacity as host had found little time for personal conversation during the service of dinner, deliberately led her a little apart when they passed out into the lounge for coffee and to watch the dancing.

"My duties are over for a time," he said. "Do you realise that I have not had a word with you alone since our luncheon at Ciro's?"

"We have all been a little engrossed, have we not?" she murmured. "I hope that you are satisfied with the way things have turned out."

"Nothing shall induce me to talk politics or empire-saving to-night," he declared, with a smile. "I have other things to say."

"Tell me why you asked us all to dine so suddenly," she enquired. "I do not know whether it is my fancy, but there seems to be an air of celebration about. Is there any announcement to be made?"

He shook his head.

"None. The party was just a whim of Maggie's."

They both looked across towards the ballroom, where she was dancing with Chalmers.

"Maggie is very beautiful to-night," Naida said. "I could scarcely listen to my neighbour's conversation at dinner time for looking at her. Yet she has the air all the time of living in a dream, as though something had happened which had lifted her right away from us all. I began to wonder," she added, "whether, after all, Oscar Immelan had not told me the truth, and whether we should not be drinking her health and yours before the evening was over."

"You could scarcely believe that," he whispered, "if you have any memory at all."

There was a faint touch of pink in her cheeks, a tinge of colour as delicate as the passing of a gleam of sunshine over a sea-glistening shell.

"But Englishmen are so unfaithful," she sighed.

"Then I at least am an exception," Nigel answered swiftly. "The words which you checked upon my lips the last time we were alone together still live in my heart. I think, Naida, the time has come to say them."

Their immediate neighbours had deserted them. He leaned a little towards her.

"You know so well that I love you, Naida," he said. "Will you be my wife?"

She looked up at him, half laughing, yet with tears in her eyes. With an impulsive little gesture, she caught his hand in hers for a moment.

"How horribly sure you must have felt of me," she complained, "to have spoken here, with all these people around! Supposing I had told you that my life's work lay amongst my own people, or that I had made up my mind to marry Oscar Immelan, to console him for his great disappointment."

"I shouldn't have believed you," he answered, smiling.

"Conceit!" she exclaimed.

He shook his head.

"In a sense, of course, I am conceited," he replied. "I am the happiest and proudest man here. I really think that after all we ought to turn it into a celebration."

The band was playing a waltz. Naida's head moved to the music, and presently Nigel rose to his feet with a smile, and they passed into the ballroom. Karschoff and Mrs. Bollington Smith watched them with interest.

"Naida is looking very wonderful to-night," the latter remarked. "And Nigel, too; I wonder if there is anything between them."

"The days of foreign alliances are past," Karschoff replied, "but a few intermarriages might be very good for this country."

"Are you serious?" she asked.

"Absolutely! I would not suggest anything of the sort with Germany, but with this new Russia, the Russia of which Naida Karetsky is a daughter, why not? Although they will not have me back there, Russia is some day going to lay down the law to Europe."

"I wonder whether Maggie has any ideas of the sort in her mind," Mrs. Bollington Smith observed. "She seems curiously abstracted to-night."

Chalmers came grumblingly up to Mrs. Bollington Smith, with whom he was an established favourite.

"Lady Maggie is treating me disgracefully," he complained. "She will scarcely dance at all. She goes around talking to every one as though it were a sort of farewell party."

"Perhaps it may be," Karschoff remarked quietly.

"She isn't going away, is she?" Chalmers demanded.

"Who knows?" the Prince replied. "Lady Maggie is one of those strange people to whom one may look with every confidence for the unexpected."

She herself came across to them, a few moments later.

"Something tells me," she declared, "that you are talking about me."

"You are always a very much discussed young lady," Karschoff rejoined, with a little bow.

She made a grimace and sank into a chair by her aunt. She talked on lightly enough, but all the time with that slight suggestion of superficiality which is a sign of strain. She glanced often towards the entrance of the lounge, yet no one seemed less disturbed when at a few minutes before eleven Prince Shan came quietly in. He made his way at once to Mrs. Bollington Smith and bent over her fingers.

"It is so kind of you and Lord Dorminster," he said, "to give me this opportunity of saying good-by to a few friends."

"You are leaving us so soon, Prince?"

"To-morrow, soon after dawn," he replied, his eyes wandering around the little circle. "I wish to be in Pekin, if possible, by Wednesday, so my *Dragon* must spread his wings indeed."

He said a few words to almost everybody. Last of all he came to Maggie, and no one heard what he said to her. There was no change in his face as he bent low over her fingers, no sign of anything which might have passed between them, as a few minutes later he turned to one side with Nigel. Maggie held out her hand to Chalmers. The strain seemed to have passed. Her lips were parted in a wonderful smile, her feet moved to the music.

"Come and dance," she invited.

They moved a few steps away together, when Maggie came to an abrupt standstill. The two stood for a moment as though transfixed, their eyes upon the arched entrance which led from the restaurant into the lounge. A man was standing there, looking around, a strange, menacing figure, a man dressed in the garb of fashion but with the face of a savage, with eyes which burned in his head like twin dots of fire, with drawn, hollow cheeks and mouth a little open like a mad dog's. As his eyes fell upon the group and he recognised them, a look of horrible satisfaction came into his face. He began to approach quite deliberately. He seemed to take in by slow degrees every one who stood there,—Maggie herself and Chalmers, Naida, Nigel and Prince Shan. He moved forward. All the time his right hand was behind him, concealed underneath the tails of his dress coat.

"Be careful!" Maggie cried out. "It is Oscar Immelan! He is mad!"

Some of the party and many of the bystanders had shrunk away from the menacing figure. Naida stepped out from among the little group of those who were left.

"Oscar," she said firmly, "what is the matter with you? You are not well enough to be here."

He came to a standstill. At close quarters his appearance was even more terrible. Although by some means he had gotten into his evening clothes, he was only partly shaven, and there were gashes in his face where the hand which had held his razor had slipped. The pupils of his eyes were distended, and the eyes themselves seemed to have shrunk back into their sockets. His whole frame seemed to have suddenly lost vigour, even substance. He had the air of a man in clothes too large for him. Even his voice was shriller,—shriller and horrible with the slow and bestial satisfaction of his words.

"So here you are, the whole nest of you together, eh?" he exclaimed. "Good! Very good indeed! Prince Shan, the poisoner! Dorminster, enjoying your brief triumph, eh? And you, Naida Karetsky, traitress to your country—deceiver—"

"That will do, Immelan," Nigel interrupted sharply. "We are all here. What do you want with us?"

"That comes," Immelan replied. "Soon you shall all know why I have come! Let me speak to my friend Shan for a moment. I carry your poison in my veins, but there is a chance—just a chance," he added slowly, with a horrible smile upon his lips, "that you may go first, after all."

Nigel made a stealthy but rapid movement forward, drawing Naida gently out of the way. Immelan was too quick, however. He swung around, showing the revolver which he had been concealing behind him, and moved to one side until his back was against one of the pillars. By this time, most of the other occupants of the ballroom had either rushed screaming away altogether, or were hiding, peering out in fascinated horror from the different recesses. The chief maître d'hôtel bravely held his ground and came to within a few paces of Immelan.

"We can't have any brawling here," he said. "Put that revolver away."

Immelan took no notice of the intervener, except that for a single moment the muzzle yawned in the latter's face. The maître d'hôtel was a brave man, but he had a wife and family, and after all, it was not his affair. There were other men there to look after the ladies. He hurried off to call for the police. Almost as he went, Prince Shan stepped into the foreground. His voice was calm and expressionless. His eyes, in which there shone no shadow of fear, were steadily fixed upon Immelan. He spoke without flurry.

"So you carry your own weapons to-night, Immelan," he said. "That at least is more like a man. You seem to have a grievance against every one. Start with me. What is it?"

There were some of them who wondered why, at this juncture when he so clearly dominated his assailant, Prince Shan, whose courage was superb and whose *sang froid* absolutely unshaken did not throw himself upon this intruder and take his chance of bringing the matter to an end at the moment when the man's nerve was undoubtedly shaken. Then they looked towards the entrance, and they understood. Creeping towards the little gathering came Li Wen and another of the Prince's suite, a younger and even more active man. The two came on tiptoe, crouching and moving warily, with the gleam of the tiger in their anxious eyes. Maggie caught a warning glance from Nigel and looked away.

"You are my murderer!" Immelan cried hoarsely. "It is through you I suffer these pains! I am dying of your accursed poison!"

"If that were true," Prince Shan replied, with the air of one willing to discuss the subject impartially, "might I remind you of Sen Lu, who died in my box at the Albert Hall? For whom was that dagger thrust meant, Immelan? Not for the man whom you had bought to betray me, the only one of my suite who has ever been tempted with gold. That dagger thrust was meant for me, and the assassin was one of your creatures. So even if your words were true, Immelan, and the poison which you imagine to be in your body were planted there by me, are we less than quits?"

Immelan's lie was unconvincing.

"I know nothing of Sen Lu's death," he declared. "I employ no assassins. When there is killing to be done, I can do it myself. I am here to-night for that purpose. You have deserted me at the last moment, Prince Shan—played me and my country false for the sake of the English woman whom you think to carry back with you to China. And you," he added, turning with a sudden furious glance at Naida, "you have deceived the man who trusted you, the man who sent you here for one purpose, and one purpose only. You have done your best to ruin my scheme. Not only that, but you have given the love which was mine—mine, I say—to another—an Englishman! I hate you all! That is why I, a dying man, have crawled here to reap my little harvest of vengeance.—You, Naida—you shall be first—"

Naida was suddenly swung on one side, and the shot which rang out passed through Nigel's coat sleeve, grazing his wrist,—the only shot that was fired. Prince Shan, watching for his moment, as his two attendants threw themselves upon the madman from behind, himself sprang forward, knocked Immelan's right hand up with a terrible blow, and sent the revolver crashing to the ground. It was a matter of a few seconds.

Immelan, when he felt himself seized, scarcely struggled. The courage of his madness seemed to pass, the venom died out of his face, he shook like a man in an ague. Prince Shan kicked the revolver on one side and looked scornfully down upon him, now a nerveless wreck.

"Immelan," he said, "it is a pity that you did not wait until to-morrow morning. You would then have known the truth. You are no more poisoned than I am. If you had been in China—well, who knows? In England there is so much prejudice against the taking of a worthless life that as a guest I subscribed to it and mixed a little orris-root tooth powder with your vermouth."

The man's eyes suddenly opened. He was feverishly, frantically anxious.

"Tell me that again," he shrieked. "You mean it? Swear that you mean it."

Prince Shan's gesture as he turned away was one of supreme contempt.

"A Shan," he said, "never needs to repeat."

There was the bustle of arriving police, the story of a revolver which had gone off by accident, a very puzzling contretemps expounded for their benefit. The situation, and the participants in it, seemed to dissolve with such facility that it was hard for any one to understand what had actually happened. Prince Shan, with Maggie on his arm, was talking to the leader of the orchestra, who had suddenly reappeared. The former turned to his companion.

"It is not my custom to dance," he said, "but the waltz that they were beginning to play seemed to me to have a little of the lure of our own music. Will you do me the honour?"

They moved away to the music. Chalmers stood and watched them, with one hand in his pocket and the other on Nigel's shoulder. He turned to Naida, who was on the other side.

"Nothing like a touch of melodrama for the emotions," he grumbled. "Look at Lady Maggie! Her head might be touching the clouds, and I never saw her eyes shine like that when she danced with me."

"You don't dance as well as Prince Shan, old fellow," Nigel told him.

"And the Prince sails for China at dawn," Naida murmured.

XXXII

Prince Shan stood in the tiny sitting room of his suite upon the *Black Dragon* and looked around him critically. The walls were of black oak, with white inlaid plaques on which a great artist had traced little fanciful figures,—a quaint Chinese landscape, a temple, a flower-hung pagoda. There were hangings of soft, blue silk tapestry, brought from one of his northern palaces. The cloth which covered the table was of the finest silk. There were several bowls of flowers, a couch, and two comfortable chairs. Through the open doors of the two bedchambers came a faint glimpse of snow-white linen, a perfume reminiscent at once of almond blossom, green tea, and crushed lavender, and in the little room beyond glistened a silver bath. Already attired for the voyage, his pilot stood on the threshold.

"Is all well, your Highness?" he asked.

"Everything is in order," Prince Shan replied. "Ching Su is a perfect steward."

"The reverend gentleman is in his room, your Highness," the pilot went on. "All the supplies have arrived, and the crew are at their stations. At what hour will it please your Highness to start?"

Prince Shan looked through the open window, along the wooden platform, out to the broad stretch of road which led to London.

"I announced the hour of my departure as six o'clock," he replied. "I cannot leave before in case of any farewell message. Is the woman of whom I spoke to you here?"

"She is in attendance, your Highness."

"She understands that she will not be required unless my other passenger should desire to accompany us?"

"She understands perfectly, your Highness."

Prince Shan stepped through his private exit on to the narrow wooden platform. Already the mighty engines had started, purring softly but deeply, like the deep-throated murmurings of a giant soon to break into a roar. It was a light, silvery morning, with hidden sunshine everywhere. On the other side of the vast amphitheatre of flat, cinder-covered ground, the Downs crept upwards, rolling away to the blue-capped summit of a distant range of hills. Northwards, the pall of London darkened the horizon. An untidy medley of houses and factories stretched almost to the gates of the vast air terminus.

Listening intently, one could catch the faint roar of the city's awakening traffic, punctuated here and there by the shrill whistling of tugs in the river, hidden from sight by a shroud of ghostly mist. The dock on which Prince Shan stood was one apportioned to foreign royalty and visitors of note. A hundred yards away, the Madrid boat was on the point of starting, her whistles already blowing, and her engines commencing to beat. Presently the great machinery which assisted her flight from the ground commenced its sullen roar. There was a chorus of farewell shouts and she glided up into the air, a long row of people waving farewells from the windows. Prince Shan glanced at his watch,—twenty minutes to six. He paced the wooden boards and looked again,—ten minutes to six. Then he stopped suddenly. Along that gleaming stretch of private road came a car, driven at a rapid pace. Prince Shan stood and watched it, and as he watched, it seemed almost as though the hidden sun had caught his face and transfigured it. He stood as might stand a man who feels his feet upon the clouds. His lips trembled. There was no one there to see—his attendants stood respectfully in the background—but in his eyes was a rare moisture, and for a single moment a little choking at his throat. The car turned in under the arched roof. Prince Shan's servants, obeying his gesture, hurried forward and threw open the gates. The heavily laden limousine came to a standstill. Three people descended. Nigel and Naida lingered, watching the luggage being unloaded. Maggie came forward alone.

They met a few yards from the entrance to the platform. Prince Shan was bare-headed, and Maggie, at least, saw those wonderful things in his face. He bent down and took her hands in his.

"Dear and sweet soul," he whispered, as his lips touched her fingers, "may my God and yours grant that you shall find happiness!"

Her own eyes were wet as she smiled up at him.

"I have been so long making up my mind," she said, "and yet I knew all the time. I am so glad—so happy that I have come. Think, too, how wonderful a start! We leave the earth for the clouds."

"It is a wonderful allegory," he answered, smiling. "We will take it into our hearts, dear one. It rests within the power of every human being to search for happiness and, in searching, to find it. I am fortunate because I can take you to beautiful places. I can spell out for you the secrets of a new art and a new beauty. We can walk in fairy gardens. I can give you jewels such as Europe has never seen, but I can give you, Maggie, nothing so strange and wonderful, even to me who know myself, as the love which fills my heart."

Her laugh was like music.

"I am going to be so happy," she murmured.

The other two approached and they all shook hands. They looked over the amazing little rooms, watched the luggage stowed away in some marvellous manner, saw the crew, every one at his station like a motionless figure. Then a whistle was blown, and once more they all clasped hands.

"Very soon," Prince Shan promised, as he and Maggie leaned from the window of the car, "I shall send the *Black Dragon* for you, Lord Dorminster, and for the one other whom I think you may wish to bring. Asia is not so far off, these days, and Maggie will love to see her friends."

Almost imperceptibly the giant airship floated away.

"Watch, both of you," Maggie cried. "I am sending you down a farewell present." She whispered to Prince Shan, who handed her something from his pocket, smiled, and gave an order. The great ship passed in a semicircle and hovered almost exactly above their heads. A little shower of small scraps of paper came floating down. Nigel picked one up, examined it, and understood. He waved his hat.

"It is Maggie's farewell gift to England," he said, "the treaty which Prince Shan never signed."

They stood side by side, watching. With incredible speed, the *Black Dragon* passed into the clouds and out again. Then, as it roared away eastwards, the sun suddenly disclosed itself. The airship mounted towards it, shimmering and gleaming in every part. Naida passed her hand a little shyly through her companion's arm.

"Isn't that rather a wonderful way to depart in search of happiness?" she murmured.

He smiled down at her.

"I do not think that we shall find the search very difficult, dear," he said, "though our feet may remain upon the earth."

Naida's lip quivered for a moment. Then she caught a glimpse of his face and gave a little sigh of content.

"There is heaven everywhere," she whispered.

A Note About the Author

E. Phillips Oppenheim (1866–1946) was a British writer who rose to prominence in the late nineteenth century. He was born in London to a leather merchant and began working at an early age. Oppenheim spent nearly 20 years in the family business, while juggling a freelance writing career. He composed short stories and eventually novels with more than 100 titles to his credit. His first novel, *Expiation* was published in 1886 followed by *The Mystery of Mr. Bernard Brown* (1896) and *The Long Arm of Mannister* (1910). Oppenheim is best known for his signature tales full of action and espionage.

A Note from the Publisher

Spanning many genres, from non-fiction essays to literature classics to children's books and lyric poetry, Mint Edition books showcase the master works of our time in a modern new package. The text is freshly typeset, is clean and easy to read, and features a new note about the author in each volume. Many books also include exclusive new introductory material. Every book boasts a striking new cover, which makes it as appropriate for collecting as it is for gift giving. Mint Edition books are only printed when a reader orders them, so natural resources are not wasted. We're proud that our books are never manufactured in excess and exist only in the exact quantity they need to be read and enjoyed.

bookfinity ™

Discover more of your favorite classics with Bookfinity™.

- Track your reading with custom book lists.
- Get great book recommendations for your personalized Reader Type.
- Add reviews for your favorite books.
- AND MUCH MORE!

Visit **bookfinity.com** and take the fun Reader Type quiz to get started.

Enjoy our classic and modern companion pairings!

Classic & Modern